SEP 1 2 2019

HORIZON

THE GAME

A small group of survivors steps from
the wreckage of a plane . . .
And you're one of them.

JOIN THE RACE FOR SURVIVAL!

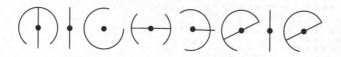

1. Download the app or go to **scholastic.com/horizon**
2. Log in to create your character.
3. Go to the Sequencer in your home camp.
4. Input the above musical sequence.
5. Claim your prize!

Available for tablet, phone, and browser.
scholastic.com/horizon

HORIZON

LIFERAFT

ADITI KHORANA

SCHOLASTIC INC.

Library of Congress Cataloging-in-Publication Data available

ISBN 978-1-338-35390-7

10 9 8 7 6 5 4 3 2 1   19 20 21 22 23

Book design by Abby Dening

First edition, September 2019

Printed in the U.S.A.   23

Scholastic US: 557 Broadway · New York, NY 10012
Scholastic Canada: 604 King Street West · Toronto, ON M5V 1E1
Scholastic New Zealand Limited: Private Bag 94407 · Greenmount, Manukau 2141
Scholastic UK Ltd.: Euston House · 24 Eversholt Street · London NW1 1DB

To all the explorers who cross into unknowns,
this one is for you.

Javi

I t was already dark by the time they saw the towers in the distance; organic and yet alien, silver spires rising from the cliff face like arms reaching toward a silent sky. They had been on the boat for hours, maybe. Then again, it could have been days. Time was strange here, not linear the way they were used to—minutes and hours acknowledged or forgotten and cataloged away. It was more like waves upon waves that crested on the shore, snatching bits and pieces back into some unknown depths.

Even without the time dilation, Javi understood how the Cub-Tones had lost all sense of time, wandering this odd place for years. It was a world that erased the past every day. It reminded him of his grandfather when he began to lose his memory. "Tell me what you ate for lunch today?" he would ask every few minutes into the conversation, because he would forget and forget and forget. And then forget again.

But there were some things that couldn't be forgotten. Oliver was gone, though they all still carried a sliver of hope that he might return, that they would laugh with him again. Akiko had drowned. Javi could barely remember Caleb's face. They had made new friends and left some of them behind. Molly and Cal were transforming into unrecognizable beings. They now knew that so many people before them had lost themselves to this ever-astonishing landscape.

Javi could always tell when Molly was thinking of Oliver. Right now she was quiet, her hand over the edge of the boat, touching the surface of the water. She turned to face her friend.

"You think we'll see him again?" she asked.

She hadn't said his name in a long time. Javi sensed that she already knew the answer but wanted to believe something different. He was willing to play the optimist. That was what coming from a big family had taught him—to sense other people's needs and to care for those needs as though they were his own.

"Sure we will," he said with cheer in his voice. "He's gotta be here somewhere." He hoped it was the right amount, not too much, not too little. He hoped she couldn't tell he was lying. Truth sometimes had to be parceled out carefully; it could wound a person, hobble them indefinitely.

Kira was huddled with her back to the shore, her knees

drawn to her chest. Since they had lost Akiko, Kira's beloved sister, Kira had gone silent. She'd barely spoken since the incident with the Colossus. Javi knew the blow of losing her sister was too much for her to take. They had been two halves of a shell for as long as he'd known them, and now Kira floated on the surface of this experience, looking lost, her eyes dark, her mood disconsolate. A part of her was gone forever.

So much had changed since the day they took that fateful flight across the ocean and arrived here, in this bizarre world. They had accomplished so much, learned so much about themselves and each other. They had survived a plane crash, the loss of friends and their favorite teacher. They had battled vicious, carnivorous tanglevine, the cruelty of shredder birds, the sharp claws and beak of the dreadful duck of doom. They'd left the greedy blood sand along with all variety of menacing robots and insects. And who knew what lay ahead?

All they sought now was to return home. This small group couldn't afford any more loss. Javi knew he wouldn't be able to stomach it.

Yoshi and Anna were talking about something quietly in a corner of the boat, and Javi couldn't blame them for latching on to each other. He wished there was something or someone in here that he could hold on to that tightly. Then again, this experience had taught him that *he* was a kind of glue himself. He knew he had united the group in times of crisis; it was a skill he had, a gift. He wished no one had been left behind, but he had done his best to keep them all together.

"Hey! Look up there!" Anna called out, and they all turned to the rising crescent of the red moon. The moons had always been symbols. They were keys to the language of this place, a language that Javi and the others had learned to navigate and speak. Red and green, floating in blue. And right now the red moon was a compass. Molly said that wherever the moon was going, there they would find answers.

"We've got to row in that direction," Molly said with conviction in her voice. She lifted her glowing arm to the sky. The more time they spent here, the more Molly *knew* things. She had learned to speak the language of this place better than anyone, but even that scared Javi. He didn't *want* to know the language of the strange machinery here, lest he become a part of it. But for Molly and Cal, it was already too late. They were hybrid beings now, not the people who had arrived with human goals and ambitions and problems.

And yet, they still hadn't abandoned their human concerns.

"Maybe we'll find him there," Molly sighed to Javi. "Maybe he managed to get himself out of the blood sand. Maybe he's there . . . waiting for us."

Javi nodded at her. After all, what else was there to do? Despite the recent coup with Hank, Molly was still, to his mind, their leader. He felt it was his job to keep her in high spirits. "Of course he's still here somewhere," he said, even though the doubts had begun to creep in. He didn't know if they would ever see Oliver again. He hoped so.

They were all tired as the boat leaped across that last torrent of waves, heading toward the barren beach. Javi was surprised at the surge of excitement he felt in the pit of his stomach. It was like they were adventurers discovering a new continent. Far from home and yet one step closer.

Finally the boat docked on the rocky beach, swaying precariously from side to side, and one by one, they all got out. Javi felt a sense of hope as he saw Molly and Cal exchanging glances. He was good at observing people, and the knowing look in Molly's eyes said it all. Whatever they were seeking, the answers would be found here. There were nine of them left and he was grateful they had each other. That they had survived this far felt like a victory in itself. He hoped they would all get out of here alive.

Yoshi

The beach and the valley and the towers ahead were monochrome. They reminded Yoshi of the surface of the moon. Though he had obviously never traveled there, he imagined it would feel no less foreign than this place. Everything here was silver and rocky. It glowed, even in the dark of the night. But a tiny sliver of light was beginning to creep over the horizon, quietly announcing the beginning of a new day.

Or what passed for a day in this place. The sun was an illusion, just as the moons were. All of it was false—just color and light meant to give the impression of an alien sky. *But for whose benefit?* Yoshi wondered. Perhaps they'd find out soon.

An elaborate city lay ahead of them, with spires that reached out in all directions. The extraordinary citadel took his breath away. Yoshi wasn't an engineer like Anna, but he could appreciate how complex this city was, how much skill it must have taken to build it. He wondered *who* had taken the time to build it, and why.

"How long do you think it'll take us to climb up there?" he asked Anna, and he liked the way she cocked her head to the side, the way the early morning light caught her eyes.

"Looks like it's about . . . I don't know . . . I'd estimate about fifteen miles from here? It's an uphill climb, so if we go about a mile every half an hour or so, we'll get there by noon. Or I guess when the sun is right above us?"

"Yeah, but these rocks don't look like they're a lot of fun," Javi added. He eyed the craggy and uneven surface below their feet.

"Luckily, we've got enough grub and water to keep us going," Kimberly said as she checked the pack she was carrying, counting the small parcels of the tuber paste, individually wrapped in leaves, that she'd brought with her.

Yoshi had to give the Cub-Tones credit; they'd adapted well to difficult conditions. They planned ahead. Kimberly always carried food. She knew where to find it, and she could distinguish dangerous plants from the ones that might sustain them on their journey. She was perhaps the most prepared and discerning of all of them. It helped that she'd been here a long time, but really it was because of who she was. She was always in the background of things, making sure everything ran smoothly.

As Yoshi scanned the group before him—Cal, Molly, Anna,

Javi, Kira, Crash, Kimberly, Hank—he wondered, not for the first time, why this place had chosen *them* to discover it. What was it they were supposed to be doing here? Throughout their journey, Yoshi and the others from Aero Horizon Flight 16 had wondered what it was that they had in common with each other, much less with a group of teenage musicians or the Arctic seal hunters whose diaries they'd found. The hunters hadn't survived this place, and yet they were fierce, prepared. This crew was just a bunch of kids with barely any life skills. How they had managed to make it this far was beyond him.

The only connection he could think of was that they were all smart, resourceful in some way. They strategized well when they put their heads together. They were adaptable. They had to be, given the circumstances. Still, he found himself annoyed when he considered his circumstances. The only thing that made this place tolerable was Anna. Her presence made everything better. If only he could figure out how to tell her that. Yoshi kicked at a single white rock amid a sea of gray ones.

All of a sudden, the ground beneath them trembled for a minute, before his eye caught a sliver of the red moon in the sky.

"What in the world was that?" Anna said. "Did you guys all feel the ground shaking?"

Just then, Yoshi heard a soft hum in his ears. He turned to look at the others and he could tell they'd heard it, too. "It happened just when I kicked that white rock."

"Probably doesn't mean anything." Javi shrugged.

"Yeah, let's keep our eyes on the prize, ladies and gents," Kimberly said cheerfully as she began to scale the rocks.

Soon, the sun was rising over the horizon as they climbed the jagged rocks that paved the way to the city. As he placed his hands on the boulders, Yoshi noticed that the craggy surface was warm despite the cool morning breeze. Looking ahead, he saw a shimmer of light flashing across the rocks, like sunlight on water, dappled and bright. He closed his eyes for a moment, wondering if he was hallucinating.

"Hey, did anyone see that?" Hank asked even before Yoshi opened his eyes again.

"That weird streak of light? Yeah, what was that?" Anna turned to Yoshi.

"Is it me, or are these rocks getting warmer? Maybe I'm just getting kind of hot?" Javi was indeed sweating, but luckily they were no longer in the blood sand, where sweating was a matter of life or death.

"Could they be heating up because of the sun?" Molly said. Her eyes were fixed on the orb of light that was just creeping over the horizon. "I mean the real sun. Since the sky is an illusion, we don't know for sure whether it's day or night. But when our plane went down, it was summer. In the Arctic, that means the sun would be out for—"

Before she could say anything else, another streak of light shimmered across the rock surface until it made its way to one of the spires. The shape began to glow as red as an ember in the morning light.

"It's a . . . I think it's a massive solar panel," Anna said. "It's powering that entire city. That spire . . . it must be some sort of—"

"It's another battery device! Look!" Javi pointed as the red light from the spire spread its way through the city. The spires glowed red for barely a second, and then, as if by magic, all the lights in the citadel went on at once.

Anna gasped. "Yoshi, you must have turned on the solar panel when you kicked the rock. It's probably some sort of switch that turns this place on."

From the wide grin on his face, it was obvious that Javi was marveling at the discovery, and Yoshi felt a surge of smugness. "That's incredible! It's so cool! It's—"

"It's a massive stove that's going to cook us!" Hank said, terror in his voice. "If we don't move fast, the sun is literally going to fry us into tater tots." His voice trembled in fear. "Move, everyone, now!"

Yoshi's stomach plunged and his legs began to instinctively climb faster. The fear triggered an immediate wave of adrenaline, which helped him navigate the dangerous rocks. With his muscles leaping almost automatically, it felt to Yoshi as though he was in some sort of video game, jumping easily from boulder to boulder. Then Kira's foot slipped.

Yoshi watched as her eyes widened and her fingers reached out, snatching at empty air. It was almost as though it was occurring in slow motion. First, her foot slid across the rock, and then her entire leg. Finally, all of her followed, tumbling forward. Yoshi didn't even realize what was happening before his entire body responded in a singular instinct. Sweat broke across his upper lip, panic boomed in his chest. His arm reached out, grasping through the air, too, until he grabbed her hand just in time.

"Kira, be careful!" he cried in Japanese as he pulled her up. "Move fast, but watch where you're going!"

"We have to get up there soon, or we'll be charred to death," Hank called out. "Everyone, speed up!"

Yoshi's heart raced. He had managed to catch Kira, but the challenge of getting to their destination wasn't over yet. And so began a race with the landscape. Their palms scratched and bruised, their faces sweaty, Yoshi and his friends panted as they climbed through the rocky incline as quickly as they dared. Yoshi's heart beat swiftly in his chest the whole time.

They helped each other navigate all the way up to the city of spires, and only just in time. As he stepped off the rocks and onto the walkway that surrounded the city, Yoshi saw a white wall of vapor rising from the rocks. He watched as a small green spider was fried to ash in an instant.

"A crematorium," he whispered to himself, grateful that they'd made their way up the rocks alive.

"This is brilliant," Anna said. "A solar-powered city. That spire must be the battery or the—"

But before she could add anything, the spire began to turn in place. It rotated around exactly 160 degrees, kicking off the rotation of another one next to it. They were both moving now, attaching themselves to a larger spire. Yoshi marveled at the strange sight before him. "It's like a motor or a—"

"It's some sort of engine," Javi said.

"That's funny," Kimberly laughed. "It all looks like a rocket ship from the future!"

Yoshi squinted his eyes. Despite their different time frames, she was right. The whole assemblage *did* resemble something out of a sci-fi movie.

"Those two spires, they look like . . . rocket boosters on a space shuttle," Javi added. "Do you guys think this is some sort of—"

By now, Cal was nodding his head vehemently, the green rash lighting up his forehead. "Controls to life raft activated. Controls operational," he said in that strangely robotic voice of his.

"This whole place is an enormous ship," Molly finished Javi's sentence for him as they looked ahead in awe. "A kind of rocket ship. Maybe a rocket ship that can get us out of here."

Molly

Molly understood things about the rift, despite herself. She knew, for example, that this place had been waiting for them to find it. Or actually, it had been waiting for her. It was as though it was practically whispering the words into her ears. She turned to look at Cal, to see if he sensed something, too, but even before she saw his face, she knew: They both belonged here. With each new day, every new rising of the false sun, they became more and more distant from the past that had once been their lives, and they were inching close to . . . what? She had no idea.

Once they stepped from the craggy rocks to the pathway that wound itself through the city, she noticed that the ground beneath her was made of clear glass. Slippery and beautiful, a ribbon of iced milk underneath their feet.

"It's the engines idling," Javi pointed out. "The heat must have melted the entire sand floor into glass."

"They would have to have been idling for years in order for—" Anna paused. "Oh." Molly could see that she understood now. The engines used to turn on every day and then idle, as though there was a giant car waiting on the curb for its passenger to arrive, hazard lights blinking. But now they looked old and slightly rusted, as though they hadn't turned on in years.

"But who is it waiting for?" Yoshi asked. "Us? Why *us*?" It was a legitimate question. *The* legitimate question.

"Only one way to find out," Molly said to him. "We open the door, climb inside, and buckle our seat belts."

"Or not," Crash said, fear in his voice.

Molly watched Kira, her arms wrapped around her waist, her eyes still dull and tired. She was standing apart from the rest of the crew. Molly was afraid that Kira had lost the will to go on. She knew what that could do to a person. She'd seen it happen to her mother, and after what happened to Oliver, she'd even sensed the beginnings of that same despair within herself. And as close as they were, Oliver wasn't family. She couldn't imagine what it must be like to lose a sister.

Molly was grateful when Yoshi turned to Kira and whispered something in Japanese. Kira nodded, then looked away. He turned to the rest of them. "We need to find the interior of the ship. Once we get there, we have a way out."

"Yeah, but this time let's stick together," Javi insisted.

Molly knew Javi was referring to Yoshi sailing off alone. She didn't want them separated, either, but she wasn't in a place to lead the team anymore. A vote had been taken, and Molly was ousted, with Hank taking her place as team captain, at least in theory.

It was a relief, to be honest. Every moment, Molly found herself slipping more into the strange daydreams that accompanied her transformation. She was too preoccupied to lead, too afraid of her own opinions, even if they weren't opinions anymore so much as strong feelings that came from her own body. It was as though this place was transmitting messages to some deeper part of her. Sometimes she simply knew certain things and she wasn't even sure how. And yet, even the knowing hadn't prevented her from making mistakes. And those mistakes had cost lives. She couldn't forget that. Or forgive herself for it.

Still, she was hopeful that they would reunite with Oliver again. It kept her going, the hope of seeing him emerge from a corner somewhere, surprising them with his big goofy smile. Sometimes Molly lost herself in the delight of this daydream; if only she could see him again, hear his voice again, know that he was okay.

As they wound their way down the glass paths between the spires, Molly had another moment of uncanny understanding. This place was more than just a spaceship. Or at least the ship was only a part of it. Everything had been built in service to something inside, like a nest around an egg. She watched the spires light and dim, light and dim, and Molly's head swam in music. Whatever this nest contained, it was the whole point of all this.

She kept her epiphany to herself.

"The spires." Anna pointed to another one, which was slowly idling before it turned off. Just then, the one next to it began to glow red, spinning like a motor. "It's a test sequence. I think they're all auxiliary engines."

More than a sequence, Molly thought with a note of glee that bordered on delirium. *A song.*

It was unbearably hot. Every few minutes, they had to duck into the shallow caves that dotted the landscape. The convenient shelters provided shade and gave them an opportunity to rest. It was as though whoever had built the city knew exactly what visitors might require when they passed through it.

"I don't know what we'd do if we didn't have these caves to hide out in." Hank wiped the sweat from his brow as he spoke.

Molly squinted her eyes into the horizon. The heat didn't bother her; her body had adapted to the rift, but she could see it was unbearable for the others. Still, she wasn't so sure that the caves were just a refuge.

As she looked out over the landscape of this new world, she felt a strange familiarity with it. It reminded her of a place she'd been reading about on the plane, in one of the travel magazines in the seat pocket: Cappadocia, Turkey. A city of stone caves and spires. In the travel magazine, there were hot-air balloons floating over the surface, like ice cubes in a punch bowl. But there were no balloons here—only blue sky and, in the distance, a large fortification made of pearly ice that glowed pink in the daylight.

They wound their way through the spire engines and caves for several hours, Kimberly handing out her leaf packets and distributing water for them to drink. Molly wolfed the purple paste down hungrily, immediately feeling a jolt of energy. By nightfall, they were nowhere closer to finding any answers.

"Systems at negative," Cal muttered, shaking his head vehemently.

"The interior of the ship isn't here." Molly shook her head. "But we have to keep looking, right?"

She turned to Hank, their new fearless leader. The boy looked haunted. His eyes were on Cal, who was walking in circles, still shaking his head. When a long beat passed and Hank still hadn't answered, Molly sighed. Didn't he *want* this?

"We'll hike to the edge of the valley and find a place to spend the night," Kimberly said, taking up the baton Hank had fumbled. "In the morning, we'll start again. No use wearing ourselves out now, when we're so close."

But Molly was unconvinced. Even though this place was reluctant to share its secrets with them, she knew it *had* secrets to share. And Kimberly was right. They were tantalizingly near.

Dispirited and exhausted, their weary feet carried them to the edge of the valley as two twin moons rose in the distance. Just below, Molly could see the ice fortification. She and Cal eyed each other.

"What? What are you two thinking?" Anna asked. By now, exhausted from a day of hiking, they'd found a small cave to huddle up in. It was cramped and a little wet, but at least they had a space to rest in for the night.

"The life raft is operational," Cal said.

"What does that mean?" Javi asked.

"That wall, the wall of ice . . ." Molly pointed. "What we're looking for is on the other side," she said. And as she did, she knew it was true.

"But how do we *get* to the other side?" Yoshi asked. "That wall is huge. It's got to be at least ten stories. And it circles this entire space."

Molly looked around at the sea of discouraged faces around her.

"I wish we still had the antigravity device," Javi said, disappointment in his voice.

"There's no way we can scale it ourselves," Kimberly said. "We'd have to be Sir Edmund Hillary to do that."

"Who's that?" Javi said.

"You don't know SIR EDMUND HILLARY?!" Kimberly squealed. "He's more famous than Elvis!"

"Maybe not more famous than Elvis," Hank noted. "But definitely close."

Molly and Anna eyed each other as Hank went on. "He's a famous mountain climber who scaled Everest."

"We can talk more about it tomorrow." Anna waved him off.

Kimberly brought out all the discarded leaves she'd collected during the day and set about making a fire to keep them warm. As the embers began to blaze, the survivors exchanged ideas about how to proceed.

"We could talk about it for days," Hank said. "What good is talking if we can't—" But Hank was interrupted by a collective gasp as Molly pointed to the dark walls of the cave, now glowing in the light of Kimberly's fire.

They all stood up, tracing the glyphs that appeared. "Cave drawings," Yoshi whispered in awe.

"They tell a story . . ." Molly gazed at the images of a city of spires, surrounded by a large fortification.

"Look at this!" Javi said, pointing to figures flying through the air. "They're people, and they're flying!"

"What does that mean?" Crash asked. "Like with that alien donut device?"

Anna squinted at the drawings. "I don't think so. They're not people. They look like birds to me, but weird-looking birds. They're enormous, even bigger than penguins." She pressed her hand against the image of one of the birds and then another hand against the image of a cave.

"If only we could still fly," Yoshi said, and Molly thought wistfully of their antigravity device, the one they'd lost. The very thing that had allowed them to come this far.

"Guys? I think I've got something that might help us." Hank pointed to a part of the glyphs that showed a depressed structure. It almost looked like a well. Down below, deep in the structure's depths, there was a glowing ring. Arrows rose upward from the ring, becoming the lines of a breeze that met the flying figures in the air.

"This whole cave drawing . . . it's a map," Kimberly said. "It's a map of this entire area. If we can just find that well—"

"It's on the far edge of this city," Yoshi said. "Close to the ice wall."

"Then we'll head there tomorrow," Molly said. Once they found the ring, they would be on their way. One step closer to the center of the nest. One step closer to Oliver.

A few hours later, when everyone was asleep except Molly, she lay on her back, eyes on the sky. She stared up at the twin moons, wondering if they were the satellites of another world. Molly knew that she was still on Earth, but this whole place had been engineered to make her feel as if she wasn't. So whose nighttime view was this? Whose sky was she glimpsing?

Yours, the strange understanding seemed to sing to her. And for once, the thought didn't fill her with dread.

After all, if this experience had taught her anything about herself, it was that Molly Davis was an explorer. Maybe she hadn't always been, but the rift had forged her into one. And now there was no turning back.

Javi

It started with an ominous bump that jolted Javi, his heart catching in his throat, and then the plane was ripped open.

A series of loud bangs sounded as Javi was pushed to the side, the terrifyingly loud whistle of wind in his ears. He was jolted again and again, his hands desperately attempting to get a grip on something—the armrests, the walls—but there was nothing to grab on to. Sweat dripped down his cheeks.

Then more chaos: Bodies flew in all directions, echoing screams of terror. Above him, the blue sky turned purple as a bolt of electric charge streaked through the broken body of the plane, straight toward—

Javi shot up with a start, panting heavily. The simple act of getting oxygen into his lungs felt like a Herculean feat. But he was relieved when he looked around him and realized he was alive. He wasn't on that plane, with the fear of death engulfing him.

Then he remembered where he *was*.

All around the cave, the others were rousing, some jolting awake as he had. Terrifying sounds echoed in the distance, instantly familiar. They were the bangs from Javi's dream. Something was cracking open, creaking like an old wooden ship, splintering and teetering and moaning in the night.

"Well, that's foreboding," Anna said.

"No, no!" Kimberly replied soothingly. "It's nothing. Probably just, you know, thunder."

"A thunderstorm? Unlikely." Anna shook her head. "More likely there's something approaching to kill us."

"It's coming from the ice wall," Crash responded nervously. He was standing at the mouth of the cave, his finger pointed toward the sky. Javi saw now that the horizon had turned a menacing green color, in part from the crescent green moon that hung ominously over the wall.

"Green moon," Anna said with an air of satisfaction. "See? That means we're in trouble."

"*Anna*," Javi muttered. "I think Kimberly was trying to comfort us."

Anna turned to him with a quizzical expression. "When we're in obvious danger? Why?"

"It's not coming from the ice wall . . ." Yoshi was already behind Crash. "It *is* the ice wall."

Soon, they were all clustered at the mouth of the cave, looking out at the massive wall of translucence reflecting back the green light. The wall practically glowed in the dark. In the real world, it might have been the size of a massive building; here, it looked especially large.

As Javi watched, a horizontal crack crawled across the wall, zigzagging its way from one end to the other.

Once again, that thunderous sound, followed by the earth beneath them shaking. Javi had experienced an earthquake only once before and it had been terrifying. Plates sliding out of cabinets, ferns leaping out of planters, door frames jumping from one end of the room to the other. This was even worse. They were being jostled by the very earth underneath their feet.

"It's breaking," Molly said, "and the engines are still running."

"What does that mean?" Yoshi asked.

Javi frowned. "If the heat from the engines turned sand into glass, imagine what it's going to do to ice."

Kimberly looked aghast. "So it'll melt?"

"And quickly," Javi confirmed. "Then it's going to flood the entire area. Anna's right—we're in big trouble."

At this grim pronouncement, Anna perked up.

"This is my fault." Yoshi shook his head. "I'm the one who turned the solar panel on. And the solar panel turned on the engines. I've killed us all."

"We're doomed," Hank whispered softly, his eyes wide.

"Look, no one has killed anyone, okay?" Kimberly said in a calm voice. "We just have to move fast. We're all going to be fine."

Just then, a large section of the wall slipped into the earth with another thunderous boom. It landed dangerously close to one of the spires. Immediately the chunk of ice splintered into a million pieces, a sunburst of jewels spilling into the air.

The moment the jewels made contact with the spire, the heat from the engine melted them into water. Javi saw mist and rain showering over the area, some of it boiling off into steam from the heat of the spire.

"You might be wrong on that one," Anna said to Kimberly.

They all braced themselves as the wave made its way across the shallow plain. Luckily, by the time the unwelcome pool splashed at their feet, it was only a few inches of water. They all jumped in terror, but Javi felt a strange calm as he stared at the ice wall.

"We have to get out of here," he said. Another crack was already forming across the wall. Even though it would be easier to scale now, it was still too high without the antigravity device. At least five or six stories, Javi estimated.

"Let's gather up all our things and head toward that well," Molly said. "If we can get that antigravity device, we can make it to the other side before there's another flood."

They were like a highly trained division of the army, grabbing up their meager belongings and wiping the night's grit from their eyes. Exhausted but adrenaline-fueled, they began the long march away from the campsite, carrying a hope for safety in each of their hearts.

5

Anna

It was midday by the time they arrived at the stone well. It sat apart from the spires, up on a knoll, with a view of the ice wall beyond. Yoshi was the first to make his way to the structure, with Kira close behind him. Anna watched as they stood leaning over the side, as though attempting to coax out its secrets.

Anna was still worried about Kira. She'd barely said a word in the past couple of days, had barely eaten.

Not that any of them were especially rested or well fed. Anna hadn't suffered the trauma that Kira had, but she still felt it every day since she had arrived here: dread. A daily— no, hourly—overwhelming panic seeping into her chest. She'd always been a little anxious. She worried about every- thing: that she'd say the wrong thing, that people wouldn't understand her. At home, a lot of the time people *didn't* understand her. Sometimes she *did* say the wrong thing.

But Yoshi always seemed to understand her. In that way, they weren't so different from Cal and Molly. Sometimes she felt that Yoshi could read her without a word passing between them. More and more, it seemed the only thing that could quell the panicky feelings in the pit of her stomach was a look from Yoshi. Talking to him, being near him, always made her feel better, like she was home again.

"I see it!" Yoshi yelled out to the rest of them. "Only thing is . . . it's a long way down there."

Javi joined Kira and Yoshi, glancing down at the well. "I'd estimate about thirty feet," Javi said, turning to the rest of them.

Anna followed and stood next to Yoshi. His arm brushed hers when he turned to look at her. She felt goose bumps on her wrist where they'd touched. She snuck a look into the dark well, and there it was—right at the very bottom— another antigravity ring, no different from the others they'd found and lost.

The ring was floating on the surface of a green liquid. Anna gathered this was dangerous, since everything green in the rift was dangerous. They would have to get the ring without touching the green liquid. But first, they had a bigger problem. Or a deeper one.

"How are we supposed to get all the way down there?"

Hank asked. "We're not rock climbers, and we don't have any tools."

"We could try to fish it out." Kimberly nodded at him.

"If only we had fishing gear." Javi rolled his eyes.

"You got better ideas?" Crash asked.

"A human chain," Anna offered up. They all turned to look at her. "The lightest person at the very bottom of the chain. Probably Kira. We hold her by her ankles and slowly lower her down using our bodies. The heaviest person stays at the top."

"That would probably be me," Crash offered.

Yoshi turned to Kira and said something to her in Japanese. Anna assumed he was translating for her, but Kira simply shrugged and nodded. She understood English well by now. Anna noticed that Kira was always listening to what was being said around her. She just didn't speak anymore.

"Just make sure you don't touch the green liquid," Anna told her, and Kira nodded again as though she understood, her eyes still exhausted and somber. "You don't want to end up like—" But before she could say it, she stopped herself.

Anna smiled then at the realization that she was getting better at saying the right things, halting when she was on the verge of the wrong ones. Sure, it was *true* that none of them wanted to end up like Molly and Cal, but she didn't want to hurt their feelings, either.

"Yup. Don't want to end up like me and Cal!" Molly said, making Anna cringe.

Ah. A bit too late, then. Next time.

The ground shook again. They all turned to look at the ice wall and Anna swallowed hard when she saw another crack zigzagging across the length of it. The panic sitting in her stomach rose to her chest.

"We've gotta act quickly," Javi said. "Before another chunk comes down."

They threw down their packs and quickly assembled themselves. Anna waited for Kira to climb to the edge of the stone well, her tiny body hovering over the wall. She looked so small and vulnerable perched there. Anna almost regretted her idea.

But they had no choice. They *needed* the antigravity device to scale the ice wall.

Anna looped her arms around Kira's ankles, and then the others helped her slowly lower her body down. Once Kira was upside down in the well, Anna followed suit. Yoshi waited for her to lie tummy down on the well wall before he and Crash reached for her ankles to steady her. But it was Kimberly who eventually grabbed on to her. And then Anna was upside down, too, holding on to Kira's ankles, with Kimberly right behind her.

"Everything good down there?" Yoshi called out.

"It's dark in here."

Anna couldn't turn her head to look behind her. All she could see was the darkness below. Slowly, she was lowered again. "Who's behind Kimberly?" she asked.

"It's me!" Molly called, and all of a sudden Anna was

plunged deeper into the well. Her heart was beating fast, but she had complete confidence in the group.

Until the earth rocked again. Anna slammed onto her side at the impact, losing her grip on Kira's left foot. Kira screamed aloud and Anna scrambled to grab on to Kira's ankle. Sweat dripped down her forehead. Her hands were already slippery and by now her heart was racing.

"What was that?" she yelled out.

"You don't want to know," Hank responded from ground level.

"I literally wouldn't have asked if I didn't want to know!" she yelled back, annoyed.

"The crack in the ice wall!" Molly yelled out. "It's bigger! So hurry!"

Anna's throat constricted in fear. There was no way to rush such a complex process, one involving their very bodies. Slowly, they lowered themselves all the way down, till Kira's arms were mere inches from the device.

"We're so close! Just one more person and—" The earth rumbled once more, splashing the green liquid so that Anna had to pull Kira back from it using the strength of her shoulders.

"There aren't any more people!" Crash called out. "Just me. I'm holding all you guys up, so grab that ring, and I can pull you out!" His voice sounded frantic and that panic was contagious.

Anna gulped down her panic. "Come on, Kira! I know you can do it!"

Kira reached her arms as far as possible, but Anna could see that it wasn't enough.

"Guys, we need a few more inches!" Anna yelled out. "Just, like, a little bit more of a stretch."

"This is all the stretch you're going to get!" Javi called in reply. "Better grab that ring quick, Kira!"

"Don't pressure her! Kira . . . I'm going to let go of one of your feet, okay?"

Kira made a whimpering sound. Anna knew how she felt: desperate and scared. That's how she felt most of the time here. Anna proceeded slowly. Her arms were burning, her shoulders screaming from the pain of holding Kira's body, even with *two* hands. Blood rushed to her face, but she felt alert, alive.

Carefully, she let go of Kira's leg, giving her a couple of inches of leverage. She grabbed tight to Kira's other ankle.

Kira descended a couple more inches. She reached for the ring, but it was still too far.

Anna called up. "Kimberly? Let go of one of my legs."

"You're sure?" Now there was fear in Kimberly's voice.

"Positive. Just do it!"

Kimberly let go of Anna's left leg, and the world lurched downward. Anna swung a little closer to the bottom of the well. By now, Kira's palms were on the ring. She carefully pulled it from the liquid. Thankfully, only the very base was touching the green goo.

"Okay, we've got it! Go, go, go!" she yelled, and Crash began to heave them up, one by one. Anna watched as the green liquid dribbled away from the base of the ring. Somehow, they'd managed to procure the one tool they needed to get out of here. A feeling of profound gratitude washed over her.

Until she heard a screeching sound from the sky.

"What is that?" they all yelled together. By now, only Javi, Hank, and Crash were out of the well.

"You really don't want to know!" Javi said.

"We wouldn't have asked if we didn't want to know!" Molly said.

"It's . . . a bunch of birds." Yoshi's voice drifted down. The swarming sound was nearly overwhelming, but Yoshi grounded Anna, gave her comfort.

"No . . . not birds," he muttered. And that was how Anna knew he was out of the well. "They're maintenance robots! They're heading to the collapsed wall!"

6

Yoshi

They *did* look like birds in the beginning, but as Yoshi squinted into the sky, he realized that they weren't birds after all. Of course they weren't. Nothing in this world was ever what it seemed to be. Silver and boxy but with wings, they were flying toward the wall.

Yoshi watched as they landed on the crack, forming a silver belt against the jagged rupture. Soon, the belt began to move, and Yoshi realized that the silver birds were silver maintenance bots; they were there to repair the wall.

"They're trying to stop the rest of it from coming down," Molly said. By now, mercifully, they'd made it out of the well, the antigravity device in Kira's hand. One obstacle down, but they still had many more ahead of them.

That was the thing about this place: It was one test after another. Yoshi knew he could manage it, but he worried about

Cal and Molly. He noticed that the green on Cal's face and Molly's shoulder glowed brighter the closer they stood to the well. It had lit up the subterranean darkness as they retrieved the antigravity ring. What was this place doing to them? If it claimed Cal and Molly, could it do the same to the rest of them?

Yoshi worried about Kira, too, though it was a relief to see her finally smiling with victory as she held tight to the antigravity ring. He was impressed with Anna as well; she was the one who had come up with the idea of making a human chain. He felt a surge of pride in their teamwork.

"Those maintenance robots look fiercer than the others," Javi said. His eyes were up on the wall of ice.

He was right. These robots had sharp beaks and what looked like elaborate tools attached to their talons. Yoshi remembered how the shredder birds were attracted to the ring's gravity powers. Would these machines attack them, too? Usually, the maintenance bots left them alone, but they also didn't usually have wings or claws. As he scanned the faces around him, he could sense that the others were having the same thoughts.

"If we use the device to scale the wall, they may attack us," Yoshi said, and he could hear the worry in his own voice when he said the words. "We should come up with a plan."

"Maybe they won't, though?" Kimberly chirped, but the others looked dubious.

"Either way, we have to take our chances." Molly shrugged. "Besides, we could use their batteries."

"We don't have any tools. What are we supposed to fight them with?" Crash said. Yoshi was getting annoyed with Crash's defeatist attitude. They were all tired and scared, but right now they had to be quick on their feet.

Yoshi wished he still had his katana. It would have been helpful at a time like this. Just as he was thinking about it, wondering if he would ever be able to get it back, Kira handed him the antigravity ring. She got down on her knees.

"What is she up to? Is she praying?" Crash asked.

"No, you idiot," Yoshi responded, smiling at Kira's genius. "She's pointing to the glass. We can crack it and use it as weapons." Yoshi smashed the antigravity ring into the ground, cracking the glass into large, thick shards.

"Hey!" Javi shouted. "Be careful with that!"

Yoshi ignored him. "There you go." He reached into the ground and carefully dug out the shards, distributing them among the group. "Glass spears. We've got our weapons."

Molly frowned down at the length of glass in her hand. "We should use cloth or leaves to make handles. Right now these weapons are as likely to injure us as they are to fight off any attackers. But they could work."

"Of course they'll work." Yoshi bristled, but he accepted the leaf Kimberly gave him to wrap around his shard's narrowest point.

"Now what?" Crash asked.

"We tie ourselves together and float as a group," Anna said, reaching for the device. "The ring has a limited radius, so let's all stick close. Everybody got their things? Their glass swords?"

Yoshi held tight to the weapon, his makeshift katana. The clear shard could slice a shredder bird in half, he was sure of it. But these robots? Perhaps he would find out.

Anna gave them all a nod as she turned her attention to the ring. "Okay . . . one, two, three, go!" she said, and suddenly they were leaping into the air. Yoshi felt a surge of excitement, adrenaline pumping through his veins. It had been so long since he was weightless. Sometimes he still couldn't get over the fact that despite all the challenges and obstacles this world had thrown at him, it had taught him how to fly.

Just as he was thinking this, the maintenance bots came after them.

"They're like maintenance hawks!" Javi said as he clobbered one with his glass sword, catching its talon with his free hand.

They *did* look like giant hawks, only made of metal and reflective glass. Their talons housed a panoply of tools—screwdrivers, hammers, knives. And their beaks looked so sharp that just the sight of them made Yoshi shudder. But he knew what he had to do. He caught sight of the maintenance hawk as it spun to the ground, cutting off the talon that held a set of tools.

"Got it!" Yoshi exclaimed victoriously. Having tools that they could use later on would be a boon. He hoped Anna was watching.

"Score!" Javi yelled, and Yoshi couldn't help but laugh.

"Grab as many tools and batteries as you can!" Anna called out.

Yoshi speared another one of the maintenance hawks through the head. He lunged forward, straining against the tie that bound him to the others, just in time to catch the battery that fell out. Before the bird went down, he ripped the tools from its talons. Yoshi noticed that the tools were held together with a piece of wispy fabric the color of straw. It was light in his hand, but oddly warm to the touch.

"This is fun!" he yelled, before the birds began to swarm them. "Anna—"

"I got it!" she yelled back.

Anna adjusted the ring, and they all dipped to the ground hard, stumbling as they landed. The birds were still coming in behind them.

"Going heavy!" Anna shouted, and then she turned the gravity up with a flick of her hand. It hit Yoshi's shoulders like a heavy load. Several of the others grunted in annoyance, but the trick had worked. Maintenance hawks smashed into pieces as they plunged to the ground, metal and glass and foam and bits of fabric spilling from their insides. Anna readjusted the dial on the ring, and the group was able to plunder more supplies.

"Okay, this time we're going for the wall," Anna said. And before anyone could so much as agree, they were flying up into the air again. The hawks took notice, but the group had their spears out; they were ready.

Yoshi heard a scream from behind, and he turned to see Kira struggling with a bird—a *real* shredder bird—that had grabbed the end of her glass sword in its beak. She was in an epic battle, trying to fight back, but Yoshi's heart plunged into his stomach when the bird wrenched the glass from her hand. As the weapon floated away, the bird struck her arm with its beak.

Yoshi saw the red line grow on Kira's arm. He turned, pushing off Crash with his legs, then stabbed the bird with his own sword. He grabbed Kira's sword before it fell out of the range of the antigravity. But it was already too late. Kira's arm was gushing blood by now, her face contorting into panic.

She's going to faint! he realized.

Before Anna had a chance to turn the dial, Kira's head fell to the side. Yoshi grabbed her wrist just as they came back down into a ledge in the middle of the wall.

7

Molly

Quick, we have to bandage her up!" Molly yelled. Yoshi had caught her just in time, but her arm was gushing blood by now. Javi ripped off a piece of his shirt, quickly bandaging her wrist. A circle of red stained the fabric. Anna checked to see if she was breathing. Kira's lids flickered for a second before they slowly opened.

"Kira!" Molly cried. "Are you okay?"

Kira looked around, confused. She opened her mouth for a moment before she let out a whimper. "Akiko?" she asked. She turned her head, searching frantically. "*Akiko?*"

Molly felt tears pricking her eyes as the memory of what had happened to Akiko registered on Kira's face. The fear fell away, replaced by a coldness that was even harder to watch.

"She's fine. She just needs a minute." Yoshi helped her lean slowly against the wall's edge. Kimberly offered Kira some water and she drank thirstily. Then she pressed her head to the wall and closed her eyes.

They were sitting at the midpoint between the valley and the peak of the wall; a shelf had formed that was just wide enough for all of them. Just beyond, they could see the maintenance robots getting to work on repairs. The sun was high in the sky now. Molly was grateful they'd made it this far, but there was still a considerable distance to go.

"There are too many of them," she said, inspecting the maintenance hawks. "It's dangerous to use the ring any further, especially with what just happened to Kira. Where there's one shredder bird, there are bound to be others. We're going to have to scale the rest of it." She looked up at the wall.

The cracks were jagged, but they formed a series of steps from the ledge to the top. They could climb these steps. It would be a challenge, given the verticality of the wall, but they could do it.

"We can use our swords as ice picks," Yoshi said. But he didn't look at Molly.

"First, let's make sure Kira is okay," Anna said with concern in her voice. Slowly, Kira stood up.

"It's going to be a tough climb, even with our picks," Javi said. He hesitated before he added, "Guys, I'm getting cold."

"Then you're really going to love what I just found," Kimberly said. She pulled apart one of the tool kits they'd plundered from the maintenance robots. The piece of fabric that held the tool kit together unfurled into a blanket as long as Kimberly was tall. Molly watched her drape it around her shoulders. Kimberly beamed in pride at her discovery. She'd made a lightweight cape for herself!

Molly wasn't cold; she no longer felt cold or heat, almost as though her body was perfectly calibrated to whatever weather condition they were in. But still, she reached for a second tool kit and pulled out the fabric, draping it over her shoulders like a cape. It was a shimmery material and fit snugly around her shoulders.

"It must be some sort of insulation material," Javi said. "These are incredible. I don't feel cold at all anymore."

"That's good," Molly told him, "because that's a lot of steps to the top."

They all looked up at the daunting wall of ice. A series of jagged inclines paved the way, but it was going to be a long, harrowing climb. The twin moons loomed above them, rising high above the wall. Always the same—one red, one green. Molly sharply sucked in her breath. They were headed in the right direction; she could sense it. They knew where to go, what to do. They just didn't know what lay beyond, on the other side.

Anna

At nightfall, they reached the silver ridge of the wall. The valley of spires and caves was finally behind them.

Anna was the first to step over, and what she saw startled her. The two moons had disappeared, as had the alien sun. In their place was the *real* sun—the sun she'd seen every day of her life—shining brightly over them.

"Where did the moons go?" Hank shrieked as the others joined her.

"We're not in the rift anymore," Molly said. They all looked out into that vast white landscape in confusion.

"We're at the North Pole!" Javi cried.

Slowly, Anna began to piece it together. She was standing firmly between two worlds: their past and their future, the valley of spires and a land consisting of nothing but snow as far as she could see. They were back in the Arctic. On Earth.

Anna couldn't help but think of home, hiking in the mountains during her summer vacations with her family. She missed her family. She missed home. The only silver lining to all this was being near Yoshi. Just then, she caught him watching her and she quickly looked away, her face burning in embarrassment. She pulled her cape tightly over her shoulders, shaking off her uncomfortable feelings.

"So, it really was Earth this whole time," she said. "But it's a totally barren landscape." Anna surveyed the space. There were no birds, nothing alive, only a sea of pure white. A sense of relief struck her: A barren landscape meant no birds—shredder or otherwise—and no birds meant that they were free to fly!

She turned to Molly, who was carrying the antigravity ring. "I guess we can use that now!"

"We can leap!" Molly said with excitement in her voice.

"But the question is . . . where to?" Yoshi asked. He was standing with his hands on his hips, looking out into the snow. The light reflecting on the ice lit up his face. Anna studied his features carefully. She'd gotten so used to seeing him that his face was more familiar to her than her own. She liked his face.

Cal pointed in the distance. "Do you see? The life raft awaits us."

"Why does he keep talking about a life raft?" Javi whispered to Molly.

But Anna couldn't see anything. Molly and Cal were no

longer who they had once been; they had strange insights to this place that none of the rest of the group had. Molly was squinting her eyes and nodding and Anna wondered what it was exactly that they saw. Still, Anna trusted them to be the compasses for this group. She was grateful for what they knew.

"We're home," Anna said aloud. The others turned to look at her. "But we're not. Not *really*. In order to truly go home, we'll have to head back into the rift. We can't survive out here, even with these capes. I vote that we follow Molly and Cal. Whatever the life raft is, it sounds good to me."

They all turned their attention back to the white plain. She still didn't know where they were headed, but Cal and Molly had that strange animal instinct about this place. Anna trusted it. She trusted *Molly*. "What now?" she said, turning to Molly and Cal.

"Cal's right," Molly said. "There's something back in the rift that's calling to us. And I think . . . I think we should find it." Her face split into a wide grin. "But I don't see why we can't have a little fun first." Anna squealed as Molly reached for the antigravity device. They tied themselves together again using the edges of their capes, and when all the knots were carefully tied, Molly placed her finger on the dial.

"Ready, you guys?" Molly cried.

"Are you kidding?" Javi said. "All the fun parts and none of the deadly consequences? I've been waiting for this moment!"

Anna laughed just as Molly pushed the dial. A tingle climbed up her spine and their feet left the ground.

"It's the only fun part." Yoshi scowled, but as he was slowly lifted into the air, the scowl transformed into a smile. Anna felt the delight of her first jump, too. She felt free as she soared through the air, flying again across that bright white landscape.

"We're flying, you guys! We're flying!" Hank yelped. "And nothing's attacking us!"

"Woo-hoo!" Javi cried. "I don't know what people do around here without an antigravity device!"

"Lucky there aren't that many people aside from us!" Anna called back.

"Make sure you look before you leap!" Kimberly yelled.

And leap they did, down the wall of ice and across the snow. They bounded over the landscape, leaving behind foot-prints as their toes struck the white earth.

"Ready?" Molly called out every time they came back to the ground, and then they were back up in the sky, laughing, losing track of time. Twenty, thirty feet into the air, landing and then flying again.

The sky here was so blue; Anna hadn't realized how different the artificial sky was within the rift. To be on the Earth again, *a part* of the Earth, was pure delight. It reminded her that they *had* to find a way back to their old lives. And that they could. There was nothing like their beautiful blue planet, their home.

Anna wasn't alone in her glee. Being back on Earth, even all the way in the Arctic, appeared to delight all her friends. It gave them hope. Javi vaulted into the air, a laugh escaping his lips every time they flew into that bright azure sky. Kimberly and Hank clasped each other's hands, grinning as their heels touched the snow. Even Yoshi looked happy.

And Molly . . .

Anna looked carefully at her now. Molly was slowing down; her jumps were less elegant, her ankles scraping the snow when she landed. Anna sprung up, her eyes fixed on Molly, and just when Molly's feet were about to touch the ground, she stumbled, and the antigravity device spilled from her hand, tumbling a few feet ahead of her.

"Molly? Molly! Are you okay?" Anna ran to her friend.

"I'm fine. Just lost my footing there for a moment." But she was panting. As Anna got closer, she noticed that underneath Molly's cape, her skin was glowing bright green. But it was more than that. Molly's face looked pale and her hands were shaking. Anna froze, a sense of panic overcoming her.

"Something . . . something's not right," Molly said. She looked dazed. Her eyes were glazed over, her face expressionless. Molly looked at Cal and Anna's eyes followed. Cal nodded once, then fell to his knees and threw up into the snow.

"Cal! Molly!" Anna cried frantically. "What's happening to you?" The others clustered around their friends, their delight giving way to abject fear at the sight of their friends struggling.

"Systems heavily burdened," Cal huffed. Like Molly, he was having trouble breathing. His lids looked heavy and his hands trembled.

"Do you smell that?" Molly asked.

"Smell what?" Yoshi said, sniffing the air.

"The air . . . It smells like . . . bread. Like . . . like moldy bread," Molly responded.

Anna couldn't smell anything, but Molly's eyes were beginning to close. Something definitely wasn't right.

Javi's eyes lit with something like an epiphany mixed with dread. "It's because we're back in the Arctic," he said soberly. "The Earth's air . . . their bodies can't process it anymore."

"That's it!" Anna said. "They're no longer . . . of the Earth. They can't tolerate the air here. We've got to get them back to the rift."

It was Kimberly who took the reins, surprising Anna. "Kira, Yoshi, grab Molly," she said. "Hank and Javi, help Cal."

The boys flanked Cal, pulling his arms over their shoulders, while Kira and Yoshi reached for Molly, whose head tumbled to the side as though she were a rag doll.

"That's the direction they were pointing in, right?" Anna confirmed with Yoshi. He nodded.

"Then that's where we're going. Get ready, guys." She picked up the device where Molly had left it in the snow and turned the knob.

One, two, three, and they were all leaping into the air once more.

Yoshi

Now he could see it—what Cal and Molly had been pointing to. It was the spire of spires, what all that machinery added up to. A giant ship lay in the distance, nestled at the very end of the rift. It looked like a sword that had cut the Arctic itself, allowing this strange, false world to fill in the wound.

They were still struggling, both of them. Yoshi was worried; they had to get Molly and Cal out of the Arctic and back into the rift.

Even though his friendship with Molly was complicated, he was worried about her. She'd screwed up a lot, made a lot of mistakes, but he wanted all of them to get home intact. And yet, how intact would Molly and Cal ever really be again? Seeing her struggle to breathe scared Yoshi. Scared him worse than anything they'd faced yet.

Molly was beginning to hallucinate. She scanned the Arctic snows, calling out Oliver's name.

"Oliver? Oliver! There he is!" She pointed into the distance before turning to a grim-looking Javi. "We have to save him! He's right there! We have to help him!" Desperation stretched her voice thin.

But of course, Oliver was nowhere to be found. Nor was that *thing* that had worn his face. All Javi could do was comfort her, squeezing her shoulder. "It's okay," he said. "Oliver isn't here, but we'll find him."

Yoshi knew that was a lie. The chances that they'd find Oliver again were slim to none, but he wasn't going to be the one to tell Molly that. As he realized this, the familiar annoyance at Molly crept back in. He wanted her to be okay, but it was still her fault they'd abandoned Oliver. She'd made so many mistakes, even going so far as to hide what she was becoming.

Still, the priority was to get Molly and Cal to safety. Once they were out of this strange and harrowing place, the blame could begin in earnest. And—maybe—the healing.

They continued to leap, stopping only to check on Molly and Cal, to make sure they were still breathing. Finally, they came upon a massive dip in the snow.

The edge of the rift.

It reminded Yoshi of pictures he'd seen of the Grand Canyon, except full of lush alien colors that were clearly not of this world. And nestled at the end was the secret they'd been hunting for all this time, the ship that would take them home. He was certain of it. It had to be.

"Do you see it?" he asked Anna, who was standing next to him. A faint smile spread across her face. The wind was blowing her hair across her cheeks, and he felt the instinct to tuck a strand of it behind her ear, but he didn't.

"It's smaller than I'd have expected," Anna said, squinting her eyes. She looked really pretty when she squinted. She turned and gazed at him in a way that made him beam. Yoshi had a fleeting instinct to swallow the grin, to keep his face still, but he fought against it. He let himself smile at her.

"The life raft will save us," Cal wheezed, and that was when Yoshi understood what Cal kept referring to. The ship they had been looking for was some kind of lifeboat?

By now, both Cal and Molly looked like withering plants. They were barely able to stand, even with help. Molly's face was a sickly shade of gray, and Cal dragged his feet when he walked, his shoulders slumped, his eyes unfocused. They were both gasping for breath. The green patches of skin on Molly's arm and Cal's face were flaky and dark.

"We have to get there quickly," Kimberly said. "These two are struggling. It's almost like the blood's been sucked out of them."

"They're like zombies," Hank whispered.

"If we can just leap down the canyon and into that ship, we're on—" Anna began, but she was interrupted by the sound of a roar so loud that they all started.

"What the . . . ?" Kimberly reached for her pack while the others clutched their glass swords tightly. Yoshi was relieved they'd kept them. Having a weapon in his hand filled him with a feeling of confidence. Then again, it would have been even better to have a plan. But they rarely had the chance to prepare for what came for them at any given time. He glanced out into the middle distance, trying to find the source of the roar.

"What was that?" Hank asked nervously. "I thought there weren't any monsters outside the rift?"

"Hunting us," Cal whispered in a hoarse voice, and they all turned to look at him.

"What does that mean?" Javi said.

Whatever it means, it's pretty terrifying, Yoshi thought.

And then he saw it.

"Guys . . ." Yoshi pointed with one hand into the distance, gripping the makeshift hilt of his glass sword so tightly he half worried he'd wear it away and slice his hand open. Along the edge of the canyon, something moved. It was hard to see. Even knowing where it was, Yoshi had to squint. And he still wasn't exactly sure *what* it was. "Something's there," he said. "I can't quite make out what it is. It seems to be—"

"It's some sort of animal," Kimberly said.

"It's camouflaged in the snow!" Hank added.

A small hill began to form at the edge of the rift, and then the hill grew and grew until it was the size of a house. The hill had eyes and a mouth. A mouth that opened wide, revealing a sharp, jagged beak. And then it roared. Yoshi's hands began to tremble. "It's a—"

"Snow beast!" Just as Javi said the words, the beast looked right at them. Its dark eyes were the size of beach balls, marbled black and blue fixed on them.

The snow beast began to run. As it approached, Yoshi could finally make out its features. It looked like it was half bear, half bird. It was covered in snow-white down, but it also had wings on its back the size of garage doors. When it roared, the ground seemed to shake. And it was barreling right toward them.

Kimberly stood frozen. "Oh my goodness, oh my—" But before she could say anything else, Yoshi yanked her arm.

"RUN!" he screamed.

They all ran against the edge of the canyon.

"Anna! Use the antigravity device!" Yoshi screamed, but Anna was too flustered, running as fast as she could. The snow beast was coming at them, faster and faster.

"If we can just get up into the air, we can leap over it!" Molly wheezed, her face ashen. She was holding on to Cal, who was holding on to Hank, both of them being dragged along. Adrenaline had awoken them, but it was a temporary fix. Neither was at their strongest or fastest.

"He's gaining on us!" Hank yelled. And the snow beast was behind Crash, roaring so loudly that Yoshi's ears rang. Faintly, he heard Kira scream, and he was shocked to find her inches away from him. Yoshi grabbed her hand and they ran faster.

Then the sickening sound of another scream: Crash's.

"Help me!" Crash cried, but the beast already had him in its talons.

"Crash!" Yoshi's stomach turned as the beast batted Crash's body from side to side. Crash's screams echoed across the snow. For the first time in his life, Yoshi's feet were frozen. He couldn't move. He knew he needed to run, either toward Crash or away from the beast, but he couldn't will himself to do so. He stood frozen as he watched it all unfold, as though in slow motion.

Several of his friends were screaming now, but Yoshi couldn't pick out their voices. He watched the beast crush Crash's body—how small he looked, compared to this monster—then raise him to its beak.

"No! Crash! *No!*" Hank grabbed the antigravity device from Anna's hand. "We have to rescue him!" He twisted the ring and the world lurched, gravity giving way. Yoshi felt himself rising into the air, saw Kira's hair dance slowly upward.

But they weren't the only ones floating. The beast lifted its bloody beak, as if responding to the antigravity. Then it extended its wings.

Yoshi gasped as the snow beast rose into the air, its great wings beating expertly within the gravity field. It lifted Crash's body in its talon, then swallowed the boy whole.

They scattered in a panic, screaming, crying. Yoshi looked at Hank, who was leaping toward the beast, still attempting to find a way to rescue his friend.

But there was nothing left to do. Nothing except survive. The creature whirled in the air, still hungry. Still *hunting*. Its eyes landed upon Yoshi and Kira.

"It's coming back!" Anna screamed. "Turn off the gravity!"

The creature surged forward, lunging for them with its thick talons. One just barely missed Kira's foot. She screamed as it lunged yet again, this time batting her away into the snow.

Yoshi turned to look as the snow beast opened its beak and roared again, its focus fixed on Kira. His heart raced. He tried to leap forward so he could help her—there was no way he was letting the beast do to Kira what it had done to Crash—but the antigravity field gave way just as he jumped, and Yoshi landed uselessly in the snow.

The creature let out a loud wail, which was followed immediately by an odd, sonorous trill.

A flute.

There was a flute playing somewhere in the distance.

10

Javi

The sound was coming from just behind him, and when Javi turned to look, his mouth fell open. He could barely believe his own eyes, but when he saw Kira with her mouth agape, tears streaming down her face, he knew it was true.

There was Akiko, riding the giant Colossus. Tiny Akiko with her flute in her hands; Akiko, who they all adored. She was alive.

"Is that—?" Molly looked stunned.

"It is!" Javi cried. "It's her!"

The last time they'd seen her, she was a small, broken body being lifted up by the cyborg. Javi remembered the moment so vividly that a small sob escaped his lips.

Somehow, she'd come back to life. Or perhaps she had never really died. It was her, with her dark hair and dark eyes, her hands gripping a slightly bent flute, holding it to her lips as she rode the cyborg. She was blasting a ghostly tune, and the giant Colossus was following her commands.

It raced toward the snow beast with Akiko on its back. The cyborg was nearly double the size of the snow beast, and it ran with force on its terrifyingly large, armored feet. Kira gaped at her heroic sister as the Colossus took a large swipe at the snow beast, knocking it off its feet.

The snow beast roared in pain, a green gash opening at its throat. Akiko and the Colossus waited until it had jumped back on its feet, touching its own wound with its talon, before the Colossus smashed its foot into the snow beast's side again.

By now, Javi was standing utterly still, and when he looked around, he realized that the others were just as stunned. They all watched the battle unfolding between the cyborg and the snow beast, each of them taking turns swiping at one another. Then: a loud roar from the beast as the Colossus pinned one of its wings to the snow.

Akiko continued to play the ghostly tune on her flute, the cyborg entirely under her control. Finally, with an odd twist of notes played on the broken flute, the Colossus lifted the snow beast in its enormous arms and tossed it away. When it finally landed, the creature leaped to its feet and ran as fast as it could.

"I can't believe she's back," Molly huffed weakly. "I can't believe she's still alive." Javi squeezed Molly's hand. Her face was grayer than he'd thought it ever could be; he didn't know how much longer she would be able to endure the Arctic.

Molly turned to Javi and whispered, "Maybe now we'll find Oliver, too."

"Maybe," Javi responded gently, though the hope twisted a knot inside him. He knew that Molly was still struggling with what had happened to Oliver. Maybe she would always struggle with it.

Like Crash. Poor Crash. Javi spotted Hank sinking to his knees in the snow, just staring in the direction the beast had fled. Kimberly stood beside him, her face in her hands.

Only yards away, the Killbots were celebrating. Kira stood with her hand over her mouth, shaking her head, tears streaming down. "Akiko! Akiko!" she yelled. It was the first time Javi had heard her speak since Akiko . . . well, since she'd *died*.

Kira ran toward her sister, followed by Yoshi. Anna trailed after them.

They'd been rescued by a ghost. Akiko had returned. It was a miracle; it was magic; it was an unexpected boon that they didn't even realize they needed. It gave Javi more hope than he had ever dared to feel in this terrifying, foreign place.

And that hope was poisoned with loss.

11

Molly

Molly felt a sob catch in her throat as she watched Kira run toward her sister—her sister, who, till now, they all thought was dead. Akiko played a trill on her flute, and the Colossus came to a stop, falling to its knees. She leaped off its back and ran to embrace Kira.

"Akiko! Akiko, *ikite iru!*"

They were jumping up and down, shrieking, sobbing, and the others came together, surrounding them, watching two sisters reunite. It was the happiest thing that had happened since they arrived here, and it had directly followed one of the very worst. The Cub-Tones stood removed: Hank, Kimberly, and Cal watching with haunted faces.

"*Nidoto watashi o nokoshite wa ikenai,* Akiko!" Kira sobbed. "Aitakatta!"

"*Daijōbu,* Kira!"

Molly thought back to the fact that it was her order that had gotten Akiko "killed" in the first place. A sense of relief quaked through her body. She felt like falling to her knees and crying. Instead, after Kira reluctantly let go of her sister, Molly reached for her.

"I'm so glad you're okay, Akiko. I can't believe you're alive. I'm so, so—" But even before she could breathe the words *I'm sorry*, Akiko grabbed Molly, enveloped her in a hug.

"It's okay. I'm fine. I was unconscious, and the Colossus thought I was dead, so he let me be. But I still had my flute. The moment I woke, I started playing it. And since then . . . it's like he's tamed! I don't know how I survived. Or why. I was lucky. I've been following you, heading to the ship, and then I waited. I knew you would come."

"The ship? You mean the spacecraft?" Javi asked.

"Life raft in close vicinity," Cal said hollowly.

Akiko nodded, a knowing smile crossing her lips. She pointed in the direction of the rift. She looked like a queen to Molly. She'd scavenged some sort of strange plant and made herself a wreath that she wore atop her head. She was draped in a cape, too; she must have caught one of the flying maintenance bots with the Colossus. But hers was white and pristine, the color of snow.

And there was something else about her. Maybe it was because she'd made her way back from death, but she was practically glowing with confidence, as though she knew and understood things that mere mortals didn't. And of course she did: She knew how to control the Colossus. She knew how to survive this terrifying place.

"Claude can take us to the ship," Akiko said, pronouncing the word like *ku-ra-do*.

"Claude?"

"After Claude Debussy, my favorite musician," she said. Molly noticed belatedly how good Akiko's English had become. She spoke haltingly, but it was clear. When had the sisters become so fluent? "He likes it," Akiko continued. "The music. *Omoshiroi*." She gestured to the Colossus. "I play for him, and he does what I ask."

Akiko reached for her flute and played the ghostly tune. It was beautiful and languid, the notes encircling Molly before they caught the wind and flew away through the white landscape. Molly felt her body relax as Akiko played. When she turned and looked at Cal, she noted that he seemed better, too. Akiko's music appeared to be reviving her, bringing her back to life. All of a sudden, she felt the air filling her lungs again. She felt her heart beating with a normal rhythm and pace. She took a deep breath. She was going to be okay. For a while there, she was scared. Now she understood that her own body responded to music, just the way everything else in the rift did, too.

Akiko continued to play a series of trills, turning her attention to the Colossus. Claude turned and fell on his back, not unlike a puppy wanting his belly rubbed. It was shocking how benign he appeared while under the spell of Akiko's music. They had feared the Colossus so much, and yet he was putty in her hands.

"Wow, you've gotten really good at controlling that thing," Yoshi said.

Akiko stopped playing and smiled at the Colossus. "He can take us," Akiko told Yoshi. "He can take us to the ship. And once we get there, I'll show it to you. I think it's the way out. But all I can do is play the flute. I don't understand how to get inside."

"How did you get here, Akiko?" Molly asked, now that she could form thoughts with greater clarity than before. "It's such a long journey. And the last time we saw you, it was at the water."

"It was a long journey," Akiko said. "I crossed the water and we climbed the rocks. We traveled the valley. Claude knew his way. I've been camping outside the ship since we came here, but I don't understand anything about it. I just know how to call the Colossus when I need him to take me somewhere."

"So you took the same journey as us," Molly mused.

"Only faster. Because of Claude. He wanted to bring me here. I don't know why."

"Administrative systems compromised," Cal said, and they all turned to look at him. "Life raft . . . the life raft . . ." He was staring right at Molly, his eyes pleading. Molly didn't understand exactly what he meant, but she had a *feeling*. The life raft was more than just a way out. It was the key to unlocking this place, a key that *wanted* to be found.

"If only Crash had survived," Hank said, his voice hoarse. Molly looked around at the rueful faces of the Cub-Tones. It seemed every time there was a victory, there was also loss.

"Rest in peace, Crash," Kimberly said quietly. Molly felt a lump in her throat.

"He didn't deserve that." Hank shook his head. He still looked as though he was in shock. "I can't believe he's gone." He wiped at his eyes.

"Why does this place keep taking away our friends?" Anna said.

Yoshi put his arm around her. "We won't forget him," he said.

"Those of us who are still alive to remember him," Anna muttered. "Those of us this place doesn't take next." She sighed. "Sorry. I said the wrong thing again."

They stood in silence for a moment before Akiko finally spoke.

"We should go," she said. Then she brought her flute to her lips and played another tune. The Colossus turned and got on his knees, holding out his hands. Akiko stopped playing for a moment, gesturing for the others to hop on. One by one, they all followed her instructions. Akiko climbed up last, sitting behind Kira. Once they were all comfortably positioned on the cyborg's back, Akiko played again. This song was still spectral and somber, but different somehow. The Colossus stood, then marched them down the canyon and to the life raft.

Molly smiled as they were carried to their destination. If they had found Akiko, there was a chance that Oliver was still alive, too. And if he was, she couldn't wait to see him again.

12

Yoshi

perture opening!" Cal excitedly cried. "Approaching absolute zero!" He kept saying the same words, with great enthusiasm, over and over again. And every time the words came out of his mouth, Yoshi got goose bumps. They were on their way, close to finding their exit out of this world.

Yoshi thought of the book he'd read once about the *Titanic*: the largest, most luxurious ship ever built. He thought about the tiny lifeboats, and how there hadn't been enough to ferry all the survivors to safety. People had died in that calamity, just as people had died when their plane crashed. It was because those who had built the *Titanic* were filled with hubris.

And what about them? He appreciated Cal's enthusiasm, but he didn't want to get overconfident. Would they all make it out of here once they arrived at their life raft? They had miraculously managed to locate Akiko, but had lost Crash. They'd lost Caleb and Oliver, too. There had been so much loss since they came here, every turn a surprise.

Yoshi wanted to return home. But he wondered if he did get out of here, if they did make it back to their old lives, whether he would ever see Anna again. He turned and looked at her and felt a pang in his chest.

Akiko continued to play her flute as the cyborg delivered them to yet another ice wall in the center of the canyon. Just beyond was the shape they'd seen from the top of the ridge. When Akiko finished her song, the cyborg bent down to let them all off. Then Akiko played another trill, and the cyborg got down on his knees and sat quietly, as though a switch had turned him off.

"He won't fit down the second wall. We'll have to do that ourselves," Akiko said. "But if you have the ring . . ." She gestured at the device before Kira reached for her hand. Kira put her head on Akiko's shoulder. Seeing them together, and safe to boot, made Yoshi feel better. "We can leap deeper into the canyon. And then we're—"

"Approaching the life raft! Approaching the life raft!" Cal said, and just as the words came out of his mouth, Anna took the antigravity ring from Hank.

"Ready?" she asked. But before any of them could answer, another roar erupted behind them. Yoshi felt the blood drain from his face. He could barely believe what he was seeing. A terrified sound escaped from his lips.

The snow beast was back. It was still wounded, with a massive gash across its chest and another on its forehead. It was even angrier than before. It bellowed so loud that the ground shook. Yoshi stood frozen as the beast charged toward them.

Akiko grabbed her flute, but it was too late. The beast attacked the Colossus from behind, shoving it to the edge of the ice wall. They all watched as the Colossus's body spilled over the lip of the wall.

Yoshi gasped. The Colossus's enormous body disappeared with startling quiet. It was gone, and they were all alone, facing the beast once more.

13

Javi

"O h no! Not again!" Javi's jaw dropped. His heart
thudded loudly in the cage of his chest. "Run, everyone! *Run!*"

The beast was still charging, faster and faster, its snow-
white fur streaked with green blood. Its enormous eyes were
furious. It opened its beak wide, the edges sharp as knives.

"No! Wait!" Molly cried out.

Javi's eyes bulged. What was she thinking? A menacing
creature—the most terrifying monster he had ever seen—
was charging right at them!

"Wait until he gets close!" Molly said. "Akiko, start playing
your flute. Startle him. Then we'll all scatter in different directions. He'll run right over the ice wall!"

Javi was unsure. "Molly, we'll die!" His voice came out a
shriek. The beast was getting closer, closer . . .

"No, we won't. Not if we time it right. It's the only way we'll get rid of him for good. On the count of three, Akiko, start to play. One!"

Javi looked at the others, wondering if in the heat of the moment, anyone would dissent. But they all looked too shocked to argue. No one had any better ideas. And the beast was a faster runner than any of them. Plus, when the anti-gravity was on, it could fly. It couldn't be outrun. But maybe it could be outwitted?

"Molly, you'd better know what you're doing!" Yoshi yelled.

"Two!" Molly's voice echoed against the blanket of snow. The beast was so close now that the ice itself shook from the force of its talons.

"Three!" she yelled.

Akiko began to play, chaotic notes that were shrill to the ear. Javi bolted right and saw his friends all running in different directions. The sound of the flute was disorienting, haunting, eerie. The beast's front claw twisted in one direction, then another, until it was sliding across the snow. Javi turned and watched as it roared in confusion. For a second, time stood still.

The beast slid over the edge. It spread its enormous wings, trying to grapple the ice with its talons. Then it was gone, and a great *BOOM!* announced its arrival at the floor below.

Javi raised his fist to shout in victory, but a second *BOOM!* brought him up short.

"Wha—?"

The earth shook. Javi could feel the ice cracking beneath his very feet. He tried to run, but it was too late. The whole wall went down, taking Javi and his friends with it.

14

Anna

I t was a silent fall, and yet still dramatic. They were carried on an avalanche of snow, descending farther and farther down the ice wall and into that white crater. Below them were the Colossus and the ship—and the prone body of the snow beast.

Anna felt a profound feeling of smallness as she was carried on a wave of snow. She twisted at the antigravity ring, but panic shook her fingers, and the ring tumbled from her hands. She just managed to snatch it back before it was lost in the white bowels of the avalanche.

Still, she was too late. Next she knew, she'd landed. Anna opened her eyes, and blurry shapes coalesced into . . .

The life raft. They had plunged hundreds of feet into the unknown, and now they were right before the thing they'd been so desperate to find: the spacecraft that might deliver them to safety, to the past, to home.

Anna was dazed when she finally rose, but she seemed otherwise unhurt. Close up, she saw that the life raft was a large construction made of sheets of thick blue glass and more metallic spires. The spires were turning, burning red like hot embers.

The spacecraft was awake; it was waiting for them.

But it wasn't over yet. Slowly and carefully, the others all rose, extricating themselves from the piles of snow that encased them. Javi and Molly, Kira and Akiko, Kimberly, Cal, Hank, and . . . Anna let out a breath when Yoshi punched through the snow, rising with a scowl.

The snow had been a kind friend to them; it delivered them softly and without any noticeable injuries. Anna brushed herself off, coughing as she felt the cold air in her lungs.

"We made it!" she cried. "We're here!"

"Approaching life raft! Approaching life raft!" Cal cried.

Just then, something about a hundred yards from her moved, a shift of white against white.

It was the snow beast, still alive, still enraged. Its beak was bigger than the flat-screen TV in Anna's living room. The same beak that had devoured Crash. Her entire body trembled as it scraped its talon against the snow, snorting loudly. Before Anna had a chance to think, it charged for her.

"Anna! Look out!" Hank shouted, but it was as though

everything was unfolding in slow motion. Anna stood there frozen, unable to speak or move. The snow beast loped toward her at full force, its eyes fierce and angry. It roared the loudest roar she'd ever heard; the noise thundered in her ears. Her hands shook and she felt tears piercing her eyes. This was the end. Anna had watched people die in this strange wilderness, had seen so many of her friends stolen from her. Now it was her turn.

She would never get the chance to go home again. She would never get to tell Yoshi how she really felt about him.

Distantly, she heard Hank's voice yelling. "NO! NO! NOOOO!!!" Then, with a flash of movement, he was there, standing beside her.

Things went from slow to fast. Anna shook her head, her eyes filled with tears. Hank grabbed her and barreled forward, dragging her along with him. The snow beast pivoted, ready to follow, until Cal's voice rang out.

"Exit danger zone!" Cal screamed. "All systems ready!" He stepped forward, splaying his arms out.

"No, Cal!" Hank yelled. But it was too late. The last thing Anna saw was the snow beast mowing Cal down, then skidding across the snow and into a molten hot spire. The engine exploded into a fireball, spewing flames.

Anna screamed. She couldn't be sure, but she thought they all did.

15

Yoshi

He's dead!" Hank cried. "Cal's dead! He's gone!" Yoshi watched as the shock on Hank's face gave way to despair. Hank buried his face into his hands, sobbing hysterically. The explosion had been so violent that there was no evidence that Cal had ever existed. His body was gone; so was the body of the snow beast. All that remained were flames and ash.

Hank fell to his knees, Kira and Akiko flanking him on both sides. The two of them knew what it meant to lose someone. And Cal had been Hank's best friend in both that old life and this new one.

"It's all my fault! He died saving me!"

Yoshi turned to look at Molly, who was watching Hank with wide eyes. For a moment, Yoshi felt terrible for her. She was the one who had given them the instruction to run and confuse the beast. Of course, she couldn't have predicted this disaster, the loss of life. She couldn't have predicted that the beast would return. And now she was the only hybrid being left among them. The only one connected to this world.

Yoshi felt a wave of anger washing over him. At the snow beast, at this place. When would they ever catch a break?

They all waited Hank out silently. Grief had become a staple of their experience here. Out in the real world, Yoshi had rarely thought about death; here, the possibility of it confronted him every day, a beast always baring its teeth at them.

They had options: They could run screaming or stare down what they most feared. Either way, death would be inevitable for some of them. Yoshi understood it in his bones. This place wanted to kill them every day—every minute, it sometimes felt like. It was a struggle just to stay alive here, and if you did, you got to mourn your friends. He felt exhausted from all the trauma, the daily bloodbaths.

Finally, Hank stumbled backward, wiping the tears from his eyes. "I wish it was me," he said. "Why couldn't it have been me?"

"Because we need you, Hank." Kimberly put a hand on his shoulder. "We need you here. We love you and we need you to be okay." But Hank was disconsolate. All they could do was wait out his grief, sitting in silence as he stared into the distance with empty eyes. Finally, he nodded, looking up at the spacecraft.

They all stood without a word, feeling the loss of yet

another one of their friends. Yoshi felt a spike of feelings he didn't know what to do with. Cal had been so enthusiastic about the "life raft," as he called it. He had been excited about the prospect of an exit from this world. And yet the valley had claimed *him*, his personhood, well before it claimed his life.

But the life raft was broken now, or at least one of the engines was. Yoshi took in the bizarre structure looming over them. It was massive, much larger than an actual lifeboat, a beautiful blue-green prism. Its walls appeared to be made of a thick glass that glowed against the snow.

If this was the life raft, how big was the mother ship? And more importantly, how would they get inside?

16

Javi

Night fell like a hush over their weary bodies, and the twin moons appeared over their heads. Using some of the flames from the explosion, they made a small campfire outside the ship. It burned brightly, lighting up their faces. For a moment, everything was still. No snow beast, no Colossus, no birds of prey or avalanches or broken walls. But death was always in close vicinity. So was loss. Loss of identity, loss of security, even loss of will at times. And yet, somehow, they always seemed to recover from the worst. They didn't really have any other choice.

It was always fairly clear what they had to do here: survive, pass a series of harrowing tests. Some of the tests felt like initiations, but into what? To this place? To this ship?

The life raft itself offered no answers. In fact, it wasn't even clear how they should *enter* the thing. It was a vault that remained closed to them. The mystery of it consumed Javi, angered him even. They were so close, had lost so much, and yet here was one more trial for them to best. Javi stared deeply at the dark, locked puzzle before he lay back in the snow, his cape draped over his shoulders, his eyes tired.

He thought of Oliver again. Javi hoped they never found him. It nearly drowned him in guilt, but Javi knew—somehow, deep down—that the Oliver they loved was gone forever. That's what this place did. It took people away, swallowed them up. He remembered the boy's cold eyes the last time they'd seen him. His robotic voice. Maybe Molly hoped that Oliver's transformation was a bit like hers and Cal's. Javi didn't think so. He dreaded the moment when she finally understood. He wasn't sure she could survive it.

"Are there any doors?" Kimberly asked, drawing him back to the problem at hand.

"You already asked that," Yoshi snapped. "We walked the entire perimeter. No doors."

"Maybe a hole at the top?" Kira asked. "We could climb through?"

"Javi already climbed," Akiko sighed. "It's a flat surface."

"Nothing there," Javi seconded.

"Maybe we have to dig below the ground?" Kimberly shrugged. "Some sort of subterranean entrance?"

"We'd have to go through snow and ice," Yoshi said, looking worried. "We could, but it would take forever. And Molly . . ."

He didn't have to say anything else. They already knew.

Now back in the rift, Molly looked a bit better, but she was still in terrible shape. And yet despite her physical frailty, Javi still thought of her as the strongest person on the team, emotionally at least. She'd led them through so much, had made the decisions that no one wanted to. Some might have been mistakes—like hiding her transformation—but it took a lot to live with one's mistakes. It took a lot more to learn from them, correct them. That process was hard, and Molly was deep in it.

Just as Javi was thinking this, he looked up to the sky at the red and green crescent moons. They were moving together, almost in a perfect conjunction. "Guys?" he said, but the others were busy trying to figure out an answer.

Kimberly sounded frustrated. "Maybe there's a secret button hidden somewhere."

Kira nodded along. "Or a key under the snow, or—"

"Guys?"

"We could wait until morning and try to start digging through the snow," Yoshi added.

"Guys!" Javi yelled, and they all turned and looked at him. "Look at the moons." Javi pointed up. Several sets of eyes looked up at two slivers of moon joining. The sky had a strange orange hue. The light was eerily fabricated, like a lamp on a deserted street.

"The sky . . . That is really something," Kimberly said.

"No." Molly shook her head, her eyes brightening for the

first time in days as she pointed to the ship. *"That's something."*

They all turned to look at the craft. At first, the symbols looked like scratch marks, but as the moons came closer together in the sky, lighting up the spacecraft before them, the glyphs became clearer and clearer. They were alien runes, written in neat lines across the walls of the ship.

These were different drawings than the ones they had seen in the caves. They were graphemes, the letters to an utterly foreign language.

"They're instructions of some sort," Anna said.

"Instructions to get inside the ship, I think!" Molly's voice was high and excited.

Javi sighed. "Even if that's true, how are we supposed to read them?"

"I can," Molly said. Javi's neck snapped around as he turned to look at her.

"They're like musical notes," she added, standing up and tracing the runes with her fingers, her head cocked to one side. She looked exhausted and depleted, but there was a hint of something more in her voice, something he hadn't heard from her in a long time: hope. "And I can read them."

17

Molly

I t didn't surprise her, that was the funny thing. None of it. It didn't surprise her that she knew how to read the notes. It didn't surprise her that they were there. It was as though she somehow knew. Her destiny lay in this moment. The bite that had changed her had always been pointing her toward this. Molly was still struggling to breathe, struggling to think, but the moment the runes appeared before her eyes, she understood her purpose. She was a part of something larger. She felt alive again.

"I can hum the notes," Molly said.

"Then I can write them down." Kimberly left Hank's side for the first time since they had lost Cal. Molly glanced at Hank, taking in his pain. He hadn't spoken at all since those agonizing moments after Cal's death. He was still in shock. She met his eyes for a moment before he looked away.

Once Kimberly had joined her, Molly scanned the wall of glyphs. Softly, she began to hum. As she did, Kimberly scrawled the notes in the snow using her fingers. Akiko picked up her flute, bringing it to her mouth, and began to play a tune. Kimberly kept scrawling as Akiko played; the music was fast and then slow, a series of trills followed by staccato notes, a repetition of sonorous patterns so different from anything Molly had heard on Earth. These notes wouldn't summon Claude the Colossus, they wouldn't fight beasts, but they all hoped that they were the answer to finding a way into the ship.

Molly must have hummed for ten minutes, maybe longer. She lost all sense of time. Electricity was coursing through her body, she could feel it. An excitement, a newness, an aliveness. She was a part of the music and the music was a part of her. She was a part of the life raft. She was a part of this place. It was all connected, she realized.

It was even possible that she was *meant* to find this place. That coming here, despite all the dangers, all the sorrow and the tests and travails, was part of her destiny. That this was a small part of her own story. As she hummed, Molly got the sense that there was more, even though she couldn't see it yet.

They were on the brink, so close to what they'd been seeking. The others watched, but as Akiko played the notes, Molly felt something changing within her. Her whole body glowed green now. She was no longer just Molly, the girl who had left home to be a part of an engineering competition. No, she was someone else, some*thing* else.

Akiko kept playing furiously, with an intensity Molly had never seen in her. This could be a major turning point for them, so some excitement was expected, but Molly sensed that there was something else driving the girl, too. Even though Akiko wasn't a part of this world the way Molly was, she had explored the edges on her own, in a way that the others hadn't. She had died and been reborn in this world. She had a special connection to it.

The others stood silently, tense with anticipation. The tune Akiko played wasn't music exactly, or any kind of music they recognized. Probably it sounded strange and discordant to them. But to Molly, it was different. It was a story, a code, a mystery. And a gateway. It was a threshold they needed to cross, and they'd cross it together.

Finally, as Molly arrived at the end of the song, the spacecraft shook and a giant door opened. Inside, all she could see was light.

Kimberly

The place was like a vision of the future. Or something Kimberly might have glimpsed in her dreams. It didn't feel real. She was mesmerized as they made their way through the halls of the ship, a series of mazes lit up in red and then green, blue and then red again. The light soothed her eyes and then it surprised her. Kimberly was watching Molly carefully, and she noticed that Molly appeared to be standing up taller, growing a little greener as she walked slightly ahead of them. It seemed as though something in her was being changed just by entering the ship.

Kimberly followed Molly, trusting her to navigate them to wherever they needed to go. She held her breath as they made their way through its luminous halls, hoping desperately that they were approaching the last leg of their journey. She had been seeking answers for so long. Now it felt as though, after all the tests and battles, after the deaths and the losses, they were finally on their way.

They arrived at a point of the maze where there were two choices: turn left or turn right. Javi frowned, perplexed. "How do we decide where to go? This place is massive. And how do we know if we take a wrong turn? We might get lost inside this crazy ship."

"It's like the Minotaur's labyrinth!" Hank cried.

"What's that?" Yoshi asked.

Anna turned to him. "It's from Greek mythology. You've never heard of the Minotaur?" Yoshi shook his head.

"We learned about the Minotaur in school," Kimberly said. "He was a mythical creature with the head and tail of a bull and the body of a human. He lived in the center of the labyrinth."

"Daedalus was the architect of the maze. Have you heard of him?" Anna asked him.

He shook his head again, so Kimberly went on. "He and his son, Icarus, were imprisoned inside but escaped on wings constructed with wax—they did okay until Icarus flew too close to the sun, but that's another story. It's a story of hubris. All of Greek mythology is about hubris, practically."

"What's hubris?" Molly asked.

"Excessive pride or overconfidence," Yoshi said, looking Molly right in the eye. Kimberly sensed he was trying to communicate something to Molly without actually saying it.

Kimberly didn't think that was fair, not to mention the fact that he was being passive aggressive. It would be better just to communicate his feelings honestly and empathetically. But Yoshi wasn't exactly good at that.

"Anyway," she interjected, "in the myth, the labyrinth is navigated by using string. So you can turn back if necessary."

"Complex technology," Javi joked.

"But I don't think we need string." Kimberly glanced at Molly, who looked as though she was sniffing the air. Her whole body was lit green inside the tunnel of bright neon blue. Was it her imagination, or was Molly changing more rapidly inside this structure? She seemed healed from her Arctic malady, at least, but there was more to it. It had brought her back to her element. The way that she squinted into the hallway, Kimberly could tell that Molly knew something. Just as she had read the runes outside the spaceship, she could read the halls of this place, too.

"Quiet, everyone," Molly said, and they all hushed into silence.

Well, *almost* all of them.

"Why are we being quiet?" Yoshi sniped.

All of a sudden, Kimberly knew what her job was in the larger scheme of things. To protect Molly, or at the very least, protect her ideas and her vision. She was the one who had to discern whether Molly's ideas were good ones or bad ones. She was the one who had to make the final decision as to what was good for this group. What would allow them to survive. No, not just survive, but thrive.

"We're waiting for Molly," Kimberly said. Right now, Molly needed to be publicly backed up and supported. Molly turned to her with gratitude in her eyes, then squinted at the hallway to the right.

"That way," she said.

"Wait," Yoshi said. He turned to Kimberly. "How do we know? How do we know whether she's right or not?"

Kimberly smiled back at Yoshi. When she spoke, confidence filled her voice. "I've lived in this world now for so long . . . technically, even longer than I lived out in that world." She waved vaguely behind them, toward the world that existed for her where she was a Cub-Tone. "I have good instincts. I know what to trust and what not to trust. And I trust Molly."

"And what if Molly's wrong again?" Yoshi finally asked. Kimberly knew that this was a knot of tension between them, waiting to be released. She was almost thankful that it was right there in front of them now, ready to address.

"Yoshi," she sighed. "Just say what you want to say."

Molly frowned, turning her eyes to Kimberly before looking at Yoshi.

Yoshi ground his teeth, then stood a bit straighter. "What if Molly *is* the Minotaur?" he asked. "What if she's leading us into a dangerous place because she's a part of this world? Isn't that a question we should all be asking? Shouldn't we all protect ourselves from danger? Molly isn't . . ." He paused for a moment until Kimberly prodded him.

"Say it."

"She's not one of us anymore. Not completely."

Kimberly flinched. She knew that they had to have this conversation, but it was still harsh to hear. And yet she understood Yoshi's mistrust of Molly. She'd watched Cal change into something completely unknowable during their time here. He'd nearly sabotaged them on multiple occasions during his fits. But Molly had *kept* the rest of them alive. And Kimberly knew that Molly still felt guilty about what had happened to Oliver. That was something she would carry with her for a long time.

Yoshi was a perfectionist. He wanted them all to emerge from this experience unscathed. Well, it was too late for that. Despite what he might think about himself, Kimberly sensed how much he cared about the others. And somewhere in the back of his mind, he was thinking that instead of Oliver, instead of Crash or Cal, it could have been Anna. Because Yoshi cared about Anna. He liked her. *A lot.* Even though he hadn't expressed that to her explicitly, either.

"Molly's made some bad decisions," he said. "Why should we trust her?"

"You're right," Kimberly said, and Molly's eyes flashed with betrayal. So Kimberly nodded at her and went on. "But *we're* all still alive because Molly's *kept* us alive. Don't forget that, Yoshi. I understand where you're coming from. I know that you're scared. But if you don't trust Molly, then trust me. *I* believe Molly. She's our friend, and she's committed to getting us home safely. The fact that we've made it this far is a big deal."

A look of understanding registered on Yoshi's face.

"We're all in this together," Kimberly continued. "I get your concerns, Yoshi, I really do. But Molly's only doing her best. She wants what the rest of us want: to get out of here. You want that, too. So let's help her. Let's support her. And let's try and work things out if there's conflict. Because all we have is each other. If we don't work together to find a way through this place—if we don't use every resource at our disposal—we're going to fail."

There were tears in Molly's eyes when Yoshi took a deep breath and held out his hand. Slowly, Molly extended hers. "Friends?" Yoshi asked.

"Friends," Molly confirmed. Then Yoshi reached for Molly and hugged her. Kimberly smiled. They were more effective when they were on the same team. And hopefully now that the unspoken tension between Molly and Yoshi had been handled, they could finally be that. But she had made a choice, and that was that from now on. She would take it upon herself to discern whether Molly's decisions were good ones or not.

"Which way do we go now?" Yoshi asked Molly, a smile spreading across his face. Molly grinned back. Then she squinted her eyes, looking down one hallway and then the next.

She took her time. "This way," she said, pointing to the left. It was a conscious change for Molly.

"You heard the woman," Kimberly said to the rest of the troop. "Looks like we're headed this way."

Yoshi

If Yoshi was honest, it felt good to make up with Molly. The combination of her instincts and Kimberly's diplomacy had inspired his confidence in the team. He sensed that they would somehow find what they were looking for.

And so they marched through the halls of light once more. A pink hall reminded him of an exhibit his mother had taken him to at the Guggenheim Museum in New York. The artist worked with light. His name was James Turrell. Like the vast spaces of the museum, the halls of the ship glowed red, then green, then blue, the color so saturated that it assaulted his senses. As he marched through the blue hall, all he could think or smell or see was *blue*, bringing tears to his eyes. And when they walked through the red hall that came next, there was a feeling of separation or foreignness from the ship, but this was where Molly appeared to be most comfortable. She navigated the red spaces with ease. Yoshi felt slightly alarmed whenever they walked through a green hall, as if a predator was watching from just beyond. His shoulders were tight until they were back in the blue halls, where once again he felt free and open.

He didn't know who or what had built this ship, but it was obviously a very advanced species. This place couldn't have been built by humans—the intelligent robots, the music, the lights, the crescent moons, the Colossus. As they made their way through the ship, the "life raft," for the first time, Yoshi felt as though he wasn't battling this world. Especially when he was in the blue rooms. He could appreciate it when he wasn't fighting to stay alive.

That was a good sign. Beyond Yoshi, none of those who were left were warriors in their hearts. They didn't enjoy the battle, but when they had to fight, they did. What made them all similar, the thing that they had in common, was that they were explorers. They were most at ease, most comfortable, when they were discovering new things. The Killbots had a natural curiosity about the world and about each other. Those of them who were left were flexible, open.

Every time they hit a turn, Yoshi watched Molly's face light up to a bright shade of green, her eyes squinting like those of a hunter seeking out its prey. "This way," she'd say. Or "That direction." He still felt himself hesitating to follow her whenever Molly gave them directives, but he was getting better, trying to release his mistrust into the bowels of the ship.

Now he turned to look at Hank. The boy's face was pallid. Hank was suffering. "You okay?"

"I could have done something to help him. To save him."

Javi put his arm around Hank's shoulder. "Hank, buddy, there's nothing you could have done. Cal made that choice. He gave up his life to save you, just as you stepped in to save Anna."

"That was brave, what you did," Yoshi added. "And what he did." He was grateful to Hank that Anna was still alive. Yoshi could understand what Hank was going through, because he knew that he'd be going through it himself, had something happened to Anna.

"Any one of you would have done the same," Hank said. "Except maybe you wouldn't have done it as stupidly as I did. It's my fault that my best friend is gone." Hank sighed. "I've known him my whole life. I don't even know who I am without him."

"Then you have to find out," Yoshi said to him. "You have to keep going."

They ventured deeper into the ship. The halls continued to glow bright light—red, green, blue. Sometimes runes would appear against the walls, but Yoshi couldn't understand them. Molly occasionally stopped to inspect the glyphs, but whatever insights she gleaned she kept to herself.

The ship was silent, save for a humming sound coming from deep within. They appeared to be moving subtly downward. Yoshi realized that part of the ship was likely buried in the ground. They were moving in spirals, kind of like the time his mother took him to the Guggenheim and they started at the top, venturing down, down, down.

When Yoshi first came here, he had mixed feelings about going back. Then he met Anna, and he wondered what it would be like to return to a world without her. But by now he understood that wherever they went, wherever they were, Anna would always be a part of his life. He was ready. It didn't matter what his relationship was with his parents, though he suspected—hoped—that they would give anything to have him back. And he missed them both, too.

Back home, Yoshi couldn't wait to be an adult, to escape the hard expectations of his father. Being a kid meant being trapped. Adulthood had sounded like a great swath of freedom.

But life always came with a set of challenges. Perhaps the ones he had faced, not just with his family, but here, would make him a better person. He was *trying* to be a better person, but it was sometimes hard.

"I'm gonna miss him so much," Hank whispered. "And I betrayed him. Sometimes it feels like I shouldn't go on."

"I know." Yoshi was apprehensive about what he knew he had to say next, but he forged ahead. "I won't feed you platitudes, Hank. I didn't know Cal—the Cal before he changed—so I can't tell you that deep down he understood how much you cared, or that he'll live on in all our hearts." Yoshi waved a hand dismissively through the air. "I believe the people we lost here are truly gone. But the fact of the matter is that, whether we're here or back at home, *no one* gets out alive in the end. Whatever you think happens after we die, treat what life you do have as precious. You let the world slip away once already, *feeling like you shouldn't go on.* For Cal's sake, it's time to shake off that paralysis. It's time to move forward."

Hank stared ahead silently. For a moment, Yoshi thought perhaps he'd been too harsh—too bleak. He should have let Javi handle the inspirational talks.

But then Hank nodded. "I know," he grated, wiping away a tear. "You're right. We've got to get home. For Cal."

They marched on.

20

Molly

"Keep going!" Molly said as they entered a red hall. She was in awe of this place, how massive it was, and yet how relatively simple. A space composed almost entirely of light! There was something magical about this ship. It presented them with runes, it responded to music, it allowed them to navigate planes of pure color. Molly almost felt as though she were journeying through a warm, welcoming sun.

She sensed they were getting closer, but to what, she wasn't certain. She understood this place at an instinctive level, almost as though she were crisscrossing the halls of her own school. Molly thought about her school: the art wing, the science wing where she spent most of her time, homeroom, the pool, the basketball court, and the track outside. She could almost see it in her mind, the space that she'd inhabited day in and day out not so long ago. And yet, she felt the same familiarity within this ship. Even though she had never set foot here before, she understood its vast hallways, the way the walls curved in around her.

"Super close, you guys!" It was as though she could sniff it. A blue hall opened up before them, its light as bright as the sky on a summer day. As she walked through it, the aura warming her skin, she knew she had found it. She placed her by-now green hands on a wall before her and watched as her fingers made imprints into the surface. The wall slowly dissolved into nothing.

Before them was a chamber. And what must have been furniture—though it looked so different from the furniture of Earth. Was that a desk? A chair? A scene was projected on the far wall, of what looked like a planet similar to Earth, except that it was flanked by two crescent moons, one red and one green. The planet was blue and green. Molly looked closely at it. The painting was animated. The planet spun slowly in space, doing a dance around its distant sun.

"It's some sort of alien planet," she gasped.

"Which means that this entire place really was created by aliens. Or *an* alien." Anna shook her head in wonder.

"But who?" Javi asked. "And where can we find them? Where can we get answers?"

"I think I know." Yoshi pointed at the corner of the room, where a large glass pod had been built into the wall.

21

Javi

Sleeping beauty," Javi said, because inside the pod was the most astonishing, lovely creature he had ever seen. It looked like a cross between a human and a bird, with a bright sheen of turquoise feathers formed into two arms, or actually two wings, covered in what looked like peacock feathers, full of mystical eyes.

The creature's own eyes were closed shut. It had an orange beak instead of a mouth. And yet Javi got the sense that it was dreaming some sort of pleasant dream, because the creature's beak was curled snugly, the feathers around it ever so slightly ruffled. Javi looked at the alien's legs and noticed they were coils of orange sinew and tendon; strong but sleek, and yet entirely regal. The alien was about the same height as Javi, maybe a little taller, definitely a little slimmer. Its bird-like face, even in slumber, looked friendly. There was a golden band around the creature's neck, somewhat like a cuff, with a black stone at the center where the hollow of the creature's throat was.

"Is it a he? Or a she?" Anna asked. "Or maybe it isn't either? A they? Gender and sex are complicated enough in our species. I guess we can't say for certain how it works for theirs." She was babbling; her eyes were wide with curious excitement.

"It's a she," Molly said, because she knew. Javi understood that she knew. "Someone from that other world. And she can help us."

"How do we get her out of that pod?" Anna asked.

Javi inspected the pod's edges carefully. It was a container made of what appeared to be thick glass. Like the spaceship itself, there was no door, no hatch, no way of opening or entering it. Simply a bird inside a globe. Who knew how long she'd been inside that case, like an exhibit in a museum? But if this world had taught him anything, it was that appearances meant nothing. There was always another way.

Sometimes, what appeared to be an insurmountable obstacle was simply something that needed to be communicated with in a different language, or looked at in a different way. Walls could be doors, if you knew the secret to the puzzle. When Javi escaped the rift, he vowed to take the lesson with him. He realized that he had something to be grateful for in this experience: It had taught him how to endure, to keep going, to push past the impassible.

He turned to Molly, hoping that she would have insights,

but she just continued to stare at the strange avian creature with an intensity in her eyes.

After a long stretch, it was Kimberly who finally spoke, looking from Akiko to Molly.

"Music," Kimberly said after her long contemplation. "Music has always been the way to open doors here. So maybe it'll work again this time."

"What music?" Akiko asked haltingly.

Molly frowned, still staring at the bird through the pod. "Maybe . . . maybe *we* don't need to open it," she said.

"What do you mean?" Hank asked.

"I think all we need to do is wake her up."

"With music," Akiko repeated, a smile spreading across her face.

"What do you think she wants to hear?" Hank asked.

Molly didn't say anything, but she pointed to the walls of the chamber, where a row of moons ran across the edge of the ceiling.

"The same song we played outside, in order to get into the ship," Molly said. "But with a few small variations."

Akiko nodded slowly. She pulled forth her broken flute, then began to play the eerie, discordant song from outside. Again, it sounded strange to Javi's ears, and maybe a little sad. He wanted so badly in that moment to go home. He felt tears pierce his eyes, his vision blurring as he watched the sleeping creature. The rows of red and green crescent moons emanated their soft light into the room.

Akiko continued to play, and the music melded with the light. All of a sudden, Javi wasn't in here, in this place. He was floating through space, his feet planted on a planet not so different from Earth, but there were two moons in the sky, one red and one green. The planet was beautiful, full of thick-trunked trees whose branches reached up into the bluest sky he had ever seen. Strange and beautiful flowers, larger than his head, blooms of magenta, yellow, orange, populated the fields. A stream gurgled just a few yards from his feet.

Javi opened his eyes with a gasp. He could see the others swaying, still in the trance from the tuneless music. They could see it, too, that strange and beautiful world that this avian alien belonged to. They might never have a chance to visit it in person, but it was real. And it looked just like the rift.

Javi turned to the creature, who was rustling beneath the glass. Her eyes opened and acknowledged him first.

22

Molly

Javi was the one who the avian creature looked at first. Her eyes were pretty and yellow. Then she made eye contact with them all, one by one: Hank, Kimberly, Anna, Akiko, Kira, Yoshi. When her eyes reached Molly, she paused, glancing at her for a long time. Molly let the creature take her in as she did the same. She noted that the creature didn't appear startled or surprised. The look in her eyes said that she'd been waiting for this moment a long time.

The creature's nictitating membrane—the thin curtains of her eyelids—fluttered for a moment. Then she pressed her wings against the walls of the pod. Just as she did, the glass evaporated into thin air. Slowly, gingerly, the creature rose up. Molly stared at her, uncertain of what to say.

Finally, Kimberly spoke. "Hello!" she said, holding out her palms. "We come in peace. Do you speak English?"

The avian creature opened her beak and chirped. Her birdsong language sounded similar to the discordant music of the rift. To Molly's ear, it was lovely. The others glanced at each other, confused, stricken, in awe. Here they were, standing before what was clearly an intelligent being from another world. It was something she couldn't ever have imagined.

The creature chirped again, looking around the room. Then she began to chirp furiously, the sounds more and more strident. Molly sensed that she was becoming frustrated with her inability to communicate. A wave of sympathy washed over Molly.

She took a deep breath, studying the creature. She was beautiful, for one thing, with translucent feathers that appeared to change colors every time the light in the room shifted. Her eyes were intense and bright. It felt like they were boring into Molly.

No, not just her. Her throat.

Molly pulled the collar of her shirt to the side, showing the glowing green of her skin. By now, the green had overtaken Molly's body, but it was her shoulders that glowed the most vividly, almost as though she might sprout wings from her upper back any day now. A shiver crawled up her spine at the thought, part fear and part something else.

The creature bowed her head at Molly, then chirped again. This time the sound was in sharp trills. Molly nodded, understanding buzzing through her mind like light-headedness. She turned to the others. "She's trying to tell me her name."

"What . . . ?" Anna asked. "You can understand her?"

Molly faltered. "I know it sounds ridiculous, but . . . yeah. I kind of can." She smiled at the creature. "The name doesn't exactly translate into English." She shook her head. "It's something like Fluttering Blue Feather."

The creature continued to chirp and Molly leaned in, listening carefully. Somewhere along the way, maybe even while she and the others were walking through the mazelike halls of the ship, she had *absorbed* aspects of the creature's language. It was like osmosis, as though the longer Molly was in proximity to parts of the alien tech, the more she learned to think and . . . and *be* like them. And the learning was quick.

"She's saying . . . something about falling to . . . the land." Molly paused. "Oh! I think she's telling us that her ship crashed."

"How long ago?" Anna asked. "How long has she been here? Does she know?"

Molly tried to mime something, but the creature simply stared back blankly. "I think I know what we have to do." Molly turned to Akiko and Kimberly. "Can you be my translators? I'll hum something, just the way I did outside, and Kimberly can write it down as notes, and then maybe Akiko can play it? That way, we'll be able to communicate with . . . I think we can nickname her Feather."

Akiko and Kimberly glanced at each other unsurely. Then Akiko turned back to Molly and nodded. Kimberly followed suit. This would be a team effort, but they were up for it.

"But what should I write with?" Kimberly asked.

"Use your finger, on the wall of light," Molly said. Then she began to hum.

Kimberly reached her hand to the wall and began sketching notes with her finger, which Akiko played. The sounds were instantly harsh to Molly's ears, but familiar, too, and the look on Feather's face said that she understood.

"I just told her that we all crashed here, too, and we've been navigating this rift, trying to find a way to get back home. I asked her if she could help us."

Feather opened her beak to respond, and a series of loud chirps emerged.

Molly listened carefully, frowning. "It's difficult to understand, but I'll try my best. I think she said 'hello' and maybe 'friends.' She's pleased we've found her. She insists that she's peaceful."

The creature went on and Molly continued to translate. "She's from a faraway . . . nest. But I think she means her planet, the same way *Earth* also means soil for us. She's still learning things . . . oh! She's a student! And part of her . . . her examination was to explore new worlds."

Molly hummed something and Akiko played it aloud. Once she was finished, Molly turned to the others. "I'm telling her that we're students, too."

Molly made a series of humming sounds, pointing to the others, trying to translate their names into Feather's language. It wasn't easy. How to turn a name like Kimberly into birdsong? She settled for crisp descriptions, one for each of them, more poetry than translation.

Javi was Warm Shelter, and Anna Eyes Turned Upward. Akiko was Gentle Nature, and Kira Shield from the Wind. She named Yoshi Lonely Talon. Hank was Carries Burden. Molly paused at Kimberly before finally naming her Storm's Calm Center.

Then Molly came to herself. She sighed, placing her glowing green hand on her chest, and hummed out a sound that meant Lost One.

Akiko played the notes and Feather nodded along, attempting to understand. When she came to Molly, Feather's head tilted, her yellow eyes blinking curiously. Then she trilled a quick succession of notes. Molly understood them instantly.

Lost Now Found.

Yoshi turned to Molly. "Ask her how long she's been here," he said.

Molly hummed and Kimberly wrote and Akiko played. When at the end of their assembly line they'd finally produced something the creature could understand, it responded urgently. Molly translated again. "It's been . . . hundreds of years. But to her, only a few days. The pod kept her still. Frozen."

"Just like us," Hank muttered ruefully. "She's unhitched from time."

"Even more so," said Kimberly. "How awful."

"How old is she?" Javi asked. Molly, Kimberly, and Akiko

did their thing again, and the creature chirped a discordant birdsong.

Molly turned back to the others, realizing that she was beginning to get the hang of this. "She says she's an adolescent. A . . . a youth."

"So she's our age!" Javi cried. "Except for all those extra centuries."

Feather chirped, this time trilling for a long while. Molly struggled to keep up, occasionally raising her hand to signal Feather to slow down. "She says she made a mistake. That the crash was her fault. She was merely supposed to explore. To watch from far away. But she went the wrong direction and got too close. Her craft got caught by Earth. It crashed into the ice . . . The entire ship shut down and put her to sleep to preserve her. She had other friends but . . . they didn't survive."

Molly lowered her eyes before she replied. "Some of our friends didn't survive, either," she said. "We lost quite a few of them. But we're hopeful about our friend Oliver." She hummed this into a tune—naming Oliver Small but Precious—that Kimberly sketched into the wall. Akiko played, and when Feather heard, she leaped up into the air and began trilling excitedly. She reached the tip of her wing to the golden band around her neck, touching the black stone at the center. As she did, a holographic image appeared all around them, filling the space of the room. Everyone gasped.

As Molly looked around, she realized that it was a

three-dimensional map of the landscape they'd traversed. The entire rift was there: the jungle, the blood sand, the Arctic snows, even the ice wall. In the forest of the far side, Molly could see the wreckage of their plane, now a burned husk. She was swimming in a map of the journey they had all taken together.

Feather chirped, pointing a taloned finger to the blood sand, and Molly nodded. Hope buoyed up in her.

It was as though Feather knew. "We lost him in there," Molly said. Feather's wing hovered over the area, and then she tapped the stone at her neck again and the whole scene appeared to be moving backward, rewinding through time. The moons sunk beneath the horizon, birds flew backward, and a troop of people—*them*, Molly realized—crawled across the landscape. First, Molly could see miniature versions of themselves outside the ship; then they were walking backward. There was the snow beast and the Colossus and Cal. Hank looked away as the explosion took place. Then they were battling the snow beast again, and there was Crash. Catching a second glimpse of the friends she'd lost along the way devastated Molly, but it also gave her a sense of hope. Feather might have answers about Oliver.

For several moments, Feather rewound through their entire story so that they could see it, too. There they were, camping at the edge of the meltwater basin with the Colossus standing guard, disappearing beneath the blue-topped trees in the Cub-Tones' makeshift compound. Finally, she saw the miniature versions of them as they marched through the blood sand. Here, Feather touched the stone on her neck again. The scene paused just as the ground swallowed Oliver.

Molly's heart was in her throat. It was an awful moment, one of the worst of the journey, but now it was suffused with hope. But as she watched Oliver sink into the ground, she could also see his body in the subterranean depths. He was struggling to breathe, screaming, calling out her name. And then he was gone.

A look of sadness touched Feather's yellow eyes. Her feathers tucked downward, pulling close. She chirped something as she inspected the 3-D map.

"Maybe the map is wrong!" Molly cried.

Feather knew exactly what she was saying, even without the translation. Her yellow eyes rose, meeting Molly's. She chirped something and Molly translated, her voice flat and disaffected. "He's gone."

Feather chirped something else, and Molly felt tears burning her eyes. "He's been gone a long time." Her breath hitched. "She says . . . she's sorry."

"He's been dead all along?" Yoshi asked.

Feather chirped something short, but Molly no longer had the will to translate.

Yoshi looked outraged. "Well, then maybe you can tell us this," he said pointedly. "I want to know why *our* plane crashed. Why *we* ended up here." Yoshi took a step forward, jabbing his finger at the alien. "Do you know why?"

Feather paused before a series of trills came from her mouth. When Molly translated this time, her voice was shaking. "The life raft," she said. "'My life raft called you here to save me.'"

Feather chirped again, and now Molly felt faint as she delivered the translation to her friends. "This chamber is the life raft. It's a pod that keeps her safe, and it will be what takes her back to her world. If she can repair it. The life raft is programmed to save her, so it automatically brings anyone who can help her . . ." Molly paused, a chill running up her back. "It brings them here," she said.

Yoshi's eyes turned dark. Molly could see that he was livid. His fingers tightened around the edge of his glass sword, and before anyone could speak or think to stop him, he was already swinging at Feather.

23

Anna

"Yoshi, no!" Anna screamed, pushing herself between Yoshi and Feather. She held out her arms.

"Anna, get out of the way!" Yoshi growled.

"No. You can't." She refused to budge, tears welling in her eyes. She knew why Yoshi was angry. And the truth was, Anna was angry, too. All of them had been pulled into Feather's orbit. A plane full of innocent people. So many had died, just to save one.

But killing her wasn't the answer.

"How dare she?" Yoshi seethed. "How *dare she*?! Caleb, Oliver, Crash, Cal . . . ! All those lives lost . . . and for *what*? So *she* can return home? What about *us*? What about *our* lives?"

"And maybe she knows how to get us home, Yoshi!" Anna stepped closer to him. "Killing her could trap us here forever!"

"And what about the others? Huh? What about your teacher, or Oliver, or any of the hundreds of others who died?"

"Hate won't bring them back! I can't see any more lives lost. I just can't. I can't take any more destruction, any more hatred. Don't you understand?" Her hand fell on Yoshi's wrist, the arm that was wielding his glass sword. Yoshi's face fell.

"We've all been through so much," Anna said. "But so has she. Hundreds of years are gone for her. No more. We've made it this far. We're still alive. We still have each other. And we're so close now!"

Then his stance softened. Yoshi looked back into Anna's eyes and he lowered the sword.

"Okay," he grated. That was all he needed to say for Anna to throw her arms around him. Her arms around Yoshi felt perfect. She understood his anger, his frustration. She felt it, too. But she also knew he didn't truly want to harm anyone.

She held Yoshi tightly for a long time before she realized that the others were watching. Anna stepped back from him self-consciously, too embarrassed to meet his eyes. She felt her face burning red hot.

Finally, Feather chirped something quietly.

Molly turned to Anna, translating the words carefully. "She says thank you. And that she's sorry." Molly squinted, concentrating on Feather's steady stream of trills and chirps. "It's the ship's automatic systems. They were searching for . . . minds. For people with the skills needed to survive and to help her.

But the systems were all . . . confused. She didn't mean for anyone to get hurt, and . . . and she wants to make it up to us."

"Then tell us how to go home," Yoshi said, his voice firm.

Molly hummed a tune that Kimberly quickly scrawled on the wall of the ship. Akiko picked up her flute again and played a series of chords.

Feather opened her beak and trilled. To Anna, it almost seemed like her eyes were bright with excitement.

Her suspicion was confirmed when Molly smiled. "She says she's going to do just that."

24

Javi

When Feather touched the black stone on her neck again, the walls slowly lit up to a bright shade of blue. Before Javi could make sense of this, projections of light, filled with symbols like the runes that covered the ship, began to scroll down the surfaces. All of a sudden, they were surrounded by complex-looking writing. Except here the glyphs were made of green light. As they scrolled past Javi's eyes, he sensed they were relaying an urgent message. Green rarely meant safety in this place.

"What are those?" Javi asked. "What do they say?"

Molly hummed the question and Feather picked up on what she was saying immediately, without requiring a translation into music. Molly was rapidly learning Feather's language just by practicing it.

Feather chirped something back and Molly turned to the

rest of them. "They're commands for the ship," she said. "Now that we've woken Feather up, she can look at all the instructions that the ship has been sending out."

"That's hundreds of years of instruction!" Anna said.

"I think she knows what she's doing," Molly said. Javi watched Feather soak up the information encoded into the runes, the symbols reflecting off her yellow eyes.

Feather touched the stone at the base of her neck with her wing. The stone lit up, turning blue, then green, then red. Feather closed her eyes, and when she opened them with a jolt, Javi sensed she'd learned something. Perhaps this was how Feather "read" information. This time, when she chirped something to Molly, Molly smiled and shook her head in awe.

"Where Feather comes from, they can download large amounts of data with a simple touch. The stone around her neck is a device that allows her to process all kinds of data at high speeds. Like . . . living computers."

Javi whistled. "My mind is blown."

"You mean it wasn't already?" Molly joked. "With the adventure we've had?"

"You call this an *adventure*?" Javi replied. It felt good to banter again. It had been so long since he'd made a joke. Every moment they'd spent here had been about survival. It was hard to be funny when you were running from snow beasts or trying not to get swallowed whole into blood sand. But now, for once, he finally felt safe.

"Do all the people on her planet read information that way?" Javi asked. He touched the base of his own neck.

Feather appeared to understand. She immediately chirped a long series of high-pitched sounds to Molly, who turned back to Javi.

"After reaching a certain age, most of their kind get a touchstone. It gives and takes commands, it processes information and decodes it, and transmits the information directly to their brains. Feather just finished going through all the data about this—"

Before she could finish, Feather began to chirp again. Molly scrunched her brow, then continued to translate. "Oh . . . Feather wants to apologize. To all of us. She knows that the life raft crashed our planes. It crashed others, too. We're not the only ones who ended up trapped here. Feather feels incredibly guilty. She says the artificial intelligence was seeking young, smart, agile minds to repair the ship and wake her. No one has been able to do that except us. *We* woke her. And now she wants to repay us. She says she's going to get us back home. On her planet, every good deed must be repaid. Every ounce of suffering is rewarded."

"That's not how it is on Earth," Javi scoffed.

"That's not how it is in America." Yoshi rolled his eyes.

Sensing the kids' contempt, Feather seemed to become unsure. Her plumage fell, pulling close.

Molly held up her hands in a pacifying gesture, humming softly.

"Tell her we could learn a lot from her planet," Javi said.

This time, when Molly hummed, Feather chirped at him.

"She thinks . . . she could learn from us, too," Molly said.

Feather's bright yellow eyes flicked in Molly's direction. Javi felt a chill descend over him. Something about the alien's glance made him uncomfortable. This whole conversation, Molly had been serving as an emissary of sorts. Like a diplomat who represented Earth. For the first time, he wondered if Feather truly meant to take *all* of them home.

"Wait a second," said Hank, his voice tight. "If the life raft needed intelligent, agile minds, then why was this place trying to kill us the entire time? Or stop us from reaching here? Why would you try to impede the very people you've dragged here to help you?"

Molly paused, then relayed the question to Feather in a halting hum. When she responded in a long, chattering trill, Molly sighed. "It's complicated. She's trying to explain it in simple language, but I'm still not sure I totally understand. I'll try. The ship had two . . . songs. Directives, I guess. One of them was to summon intelligent beings to help, if that was possible. And the second was to make this place safe for her, in case help didn't arrive in time. I suppose we'd call that xenoforming. It created a miniature version of her world, here in the Arctic. But the problem is that both these directives were left running unattended for hundreds of years. And eventually, they ended up in conflict."

"The two factions," Javi whispered, his voice raw. "That's

why we saw the tech fighting itself. It's why parts of this place seemed to be urging us forward, while others held us back."

This time Molly nodded without consulting Feather. It was like she knew. "Part of the problem is that nature is impossible to control. But the conflict between the two directives must have been so severe that the xenoforming directive fought the other as it tried to help any helpers who crossed the biomes. It wanted to keep the biomes uncontaminated."

Something struck Javi then. "Because we were—"

"Because *we* were considered the aliens."

Javi felt the floor tremble, an almost imperceptible vibration that ran up his feet.

Feather chirped something, and Molly's eyes widened.

"Oh no . . ." Javi said. "I can tell that's gonna be something bad."

"Can't we get a moment of peace here?" Yoshi grumbled.

"I think . . ." Molly said slowly, "that we got here just in time." She pointed to the holographic map. "The ice walls have started crumbling. Soon, they'll all come down. And when that happens, this place will flood and get submerged into the ocean. There's nothing we can do to stop it, but we *can* fix the ship and get out of here. And if we do, you get to go home. And so does Feather."

You? Javi thought. His stomach twisted. What did she mean by *you*?

"We can fix the ship," Molly said, placing a finger thoughtfully to her lips. "But it'll take all of us to do that."

Javi looked at the others. Anna was the one who nodded first, but Javi quickly followed. Then Kira and Akiko, then Yoshi, and finally Hank and Kimberly. They had no choice. All they wanted was to return home.

All of them.

25

Anna

Feather's chirp sounded especially frantic when Molly translated her next string of trills. Even Molly looked concerned.

"We saw the state of the valley walls," she said. "They're going to collapse, burying the whole rift. We have to get out *now*, before that happens. There's just one problem. The ship won't fly."

"Why not?" Anna asked.

Molly turned to Feather, humming softly, and the young alien replied in a long, complicated canticle of birdsong. Anna glanced at Molly, expecting her to look as overwhelmed as Anna felt. Instead, Molly nodded along, understanding sharpening her expression.

"The life raft's been buried here for hundreds of years,

melting the ice and then refreezing it." She shook her head. "In short, we're stuck. But even beyond that, the ship is damaged. The explosion that killed Cal also scorched the hull."

Hank ran a hand through his hair. "How . . . how do we possibly fix those problems?"

Anna smiled. "By being engineers."

Molly grinned at her, and Javi let out a little *whoop* of excitement.

"Okay, then," Molly said. "Theories? Conjectures?"

"First, we'll need to shut down the environmental controls," Anna said. "So that as of this moment, the biomes stop fighting us."

"But maybe we could use them?" Kimberly said. "Like how Akiko was able to use the Colossus."

Akiko's eyes brightened at the same moment Molly's did.

"Of course," Molly said. "The Colossus. We could use it to repair the ship."

"That," Javi said, "plus the maintenance bots for finer issues and soldering. Now that Feather is awake, maybe she can direct them away from killing us and back to fixing what's broken."

While Molly explained their idea to Feather—the alien's yellow eyes bright as she listened, her head tilting curiously from side to side—Yoshi frowned at the colored panes all around them.

"It won't be enough," he said. "The ship is still trapped in the ice. We've walked through this whole thing. It's huge. Not even the Colossus is that strong."

Anna held up the alien device—the ring covered in runes. She'd managed to save it from the snowy clutches of the avalanche. "If only we could use this on the whole ship."

As soon as she saw the ring, Feather began trilling excitedly. She rushed to Molly, her movements light and buoyant. Watching her move, it seemed to Anna that a stiff wind might blow the alien away. Molly grinned as she listened, then turned to Anna.

"Your wish is granted."

The next hour was a flurry of activity. Akiko, Kimberly, and Kira left the ship, where Akiko used her broken flute to awaken the buried Colossus. She then coerced him into pulling spare materials from the nearby spires to patch the life raft's hull. Watching the work outside from the light-pane walls inside the ship, Anna thought the Colossus looked like the largest handyman on Earth, if not the galaxy.

Apparently, regaining a degree of control over the rogue environmental functions was a complicated process. Feather spent nearly the full hour manipulating the holographic map with her talon-like appendages. Like human hands, Feather's species had developed opposable digits that were perfect for tool manipulation. Of course, all birds on Earth had finger bones, too; most were just hidden within the wings, essential for flight control. Feather's, though, were bare, and able to perform intricate tasks. Anna wondered if that meant her species had lost the ability to fly under their own power, or if they'd ever had it. Perhaps that's what the antigravity devices were for.

In short, Anna was fascinated. She tried not to stare *too* much.

Finally, Feather chirped, and the hologram shifted, the field of data tessellating into a new abstract image, like a kaleidoscope. Anna saw several small shapes appearing along the edge of the window-like pane of light.

"The maintenance drones are here," she said.

"Here comes the creepy, robotic cavalry," Javi agreed nervously. "They *are* here to help us, right?"

They all watched as the mites swarmed past Akiko, Kira, and Kimberly, toward the ship's exterior. Antennae extended, they quickly set to work fastening the panes the Colossus had collected.

"That's one problem down," Hank said. "And one to go."

"Feather can help with that, too," Molly said, the relief palpable in her voice. "Normally, the physics-bending technology in these rings only works in a small range. But the life raft was designed to amplify it. If we sync the ring we have to the ship, it can use any of the settings—and even magnify them."

"That's brilliant!" Anna cried out. "It's the most amazing technology I've ever heard of."

"Alien technology," Javi joked. "We should all be so lucky to get our hands on it."

"It's the least the aliens can do for us," Yoshi grumbled.

Anna held the antigravity device in her hand, her fingers running lightly over the symbols. She wondered if technology like this would ever exist on Earth. It could solve so many problems, and likely create a few more. Still, it was wondrous.

"Where are we with the ship?" Molly asked.

They could still see Akiko playing her flute as the Colossus finished working on the hull. Feather touched her wing to the hologram and the image lit up to a shade of blue.

"It works!" Molly cried.

Anna stepped forward, extending her hand toward Feather. Gripped in her palm was the alien ring. Feather took it, her nictitating membrane blinking. She set the ring within the hologram, and the whole shape changed again. Anna stepped back toward Yoshi. She watched the physical display of information shift and dance, completely unable to read what it was depicting, but still enjoying the show.

Without realizing she was doing it, Anna reached for Yoshi's hand and squeezed it. She felt brave for a moment. She knew she wasn't always good with words, but there were specific ones she needed to say to Yoshi. "Whatever happens," she said to him, "I'm glad you're here with me. I'm glad we met. I'm glad we were in this together."

"Me too," he said. Anna was too afraid to look at Yoshi's

face, but from the tone of his voice, she could tell he was smiling. He squeezed her hand back. "You're the best thing about this whole place. And if we get stuck here—"

"We won't," Anna said.

"How do you know?"

She wasn't completely sure. But she had to believe. They had made it this far, after all, hadn't they? She had learned so much about herself. At the beginning of this journey, she couldn't ever have imagined holding Yoshi's hand and telling him something so close to her heart. But she had. This adventure had changed her. It had made her believe that change was possible. And it was. She was proof of it.

Slowly, a series of seats emerged from the ground, forming a circle. Nine seats, which, she gathered, were for them: Javi, Molly, Yoshi, Akiko, Kira, Hank, Kimberly, and Anna. And one for Feather, in the center.

Anna looked at Yoshi in shock. "I think that means we're going home."

"You were right," he said.

"I guess I am . . . sometimes," she said, smiling at him.

When Akiko and the others returned to the ship, all of them took to their seats. Belts emerged around their waists.

From the hologram came a series of chirps. Molly translated. "Feather is going to activate the gravity setting, along with the ship's power. It should be enough to lift us out, but it could also set off a reaction that collapses the area. Maybe the whole rift."

"What about the rest of the Cub-Tones?" Hank asked. "Dana and the others? We've got to get them before we take off!"

Molly nodded. "We're going to. But we'll have to act quickly." She glanced to Feather, humming in her musical language. "On the count of three, we'll activate the gravity setting and get our friends. Hold tight! One . . . two . . ."

26

Javi

Javi felt the floor move below him, but then he realized that there was no floor . . .

"What the—" Javi could barely get the words out before he heard the blast of engines, and all of a sudden, they were all suspended in air. An instinctive gasp emerged from his mouth, and his hands trembled when he realized that they were simply floating in their seats.

The center of the life raft appeared to be made of clear glass, or a substance like it. The walls of light had shifted to reveal the view directly outside the ship. Underneath their feet, Javi could see the valley below. His hands shook as he was reminded of the last time he was flying inside an aircraft: the plane that had crashed.

"Don't panic, don't panic," he whispered to himself.

Molly placed a hand on his shoulder. "It's okay," she said. "We're going to be fine."

"How do you know? Have you ever been inside one of these things before?"

"No, but I think Feather and her civilization are pretty advanced. She knows what she's doing."

"Yeah," Javi muttered. "So advanced that she crashed a ship in the Arctic and it held us all hostage."

"Well. Yes," Molly said. "But we should let her make it up to us. Just try to enjoy the ride."

Javi attempted to smile. "I guess I don't know the next time I'll be up in an alien spacecraft in the future, huh?" Molly grinned in response. Javi might have been imagining it, but her smile seemed a little sad.

In the center of the circle, a suspended screen showed the entire valley.

Feather chirped something to Molly, who turned to the others. "Hold tight. We're going to grab the rest of the Cub-Tones. This next bit will be *fast*." In the hologram, Javi watched one side of the ice wall collapse below them. It broke into a series of white fragments. Javi whimpered in fear.

The ship shot up in the air quickly. Across from Javi, Yoshi reached for Anna, grabbing her hand. In the projection, the ice began to melt, flooding a large section of the rift. Though it was rendered in miniature, Javi knew that tidal wave was big enough to sweep the entire region.

And before he could even process what a wave that size might look like in person, he saw it—water flooding beneath the false-glass walls of the ship. Another section of the ice came down in the projection, leaving only one last fortification. The sound of it crashing was thunderous. Millions of pieces splintered off, melting into the valley floor. There was a violence to it, and yet Javi felt gratified that this place, which had trapped so many people within it, was ending. They could all finally be free.

"Hang on to each other!" Molly cried as the ship dipped through the valley and back up into the air again. Suddenly, the scenes of the valley gave way to Arctic white. Javi watched as the tidal wave below them swept the rift. The last piece of the ice wall came down, taking the white landscape with it. All that was left was a small ocean.

Still, they flew. Faster and faster, back into the valley. Over the hills and the desert and the plains as the wave followed closely behind.

"There!" Hank cried, pointing toward a vast swath of eerie blue trees. "That's the forest where our encampment is!"

Javi wondered how they would find the compound amid all that forest, but apparently the ship's computer had already done the work. There was a jolt that shook the entire structure, and then, to Javi's shock, he saw them. Dana and the others were perched on the edge of the forest. They were still at the old campsite, sitting around a fire and staring up at the ship with expressions of utter disbelief. Unbeknownst to them, this entire world was about to come undone.

There were Dana and Pammy, Stu and Drew. Javi felt relieved to see their faces again. The ship dipped closer and they stood up, holding their makeshift weapons in their hands.

The projection in the center of the circle shifted so that Javi and the others could see the outer doors opening for the Cub-Tones.

"Dana!" Kimberly cried. "We've come to rescue you!" They all heard her voice reverberating outside the ship.

"We found a way to get out of here!" Javi yelled out to them.

"What is that?" Dana shouted. Her voiced echoed in the control room. "I'm not going anywhere in that thing!"

Stu looked stunned. "Whoa! A flying ship! It's like an alien—"

"It's an alien spaceship!" Drew cried.

"Looks kinda scary to me," Pammy said as she clenched her hands into nervous fists.

"It's fun, I promise!" Javi said. He was finally getting the hang of flying in this thing.

"Dana, the whole valley is going to collapse any second now," Molly said. "If you want to survive, get in this space-craft *now*."

Dana and the others turned to look behind them. The tidal wave was cresting above the tops of the trees. Dana's mouth went slack, and before she had a chance to say anything, Stu and Drew were already bounding toward the ship.

Pammy and Dana bolted after them.

Drew and Stu grabbed their hands and pulled the other Cub-Tones into the ship, just as the outer doors slammed shut. The ship shuddered and shot into the air, propelling Javi's stomach down to his feet. Four more seats popped up from the floor just as Dana and the others made their way into the control room, their faces bewildered.

"Better sit down for this," said Hank.

They flew higher and higher up, above the Arctic, above the Earth. Below, Javi could see the biomes destroyed, an entire world decimated. Forests were submerged underneath the tide. The desert they had traversed, the basin they had crossed in their makeshift boats. The spires and the caves. All of it was gone now. The wave took it all—the land they had navigated for weeks, the robots and the plants, the trees and the blood sand. The Arctic snows and the Colossus and the wreckage of their plane.

It also took those who they had lost. Caleb and Oliver and Crash and Cal. All the people who hadn't survived that fateful plane crash.

But *they* were still alive. And they were free. All that was left of this place was their memories of it; memories they would carry with them forever. Stories they would tell their families, if and when they managed to make it home safely. Javi was beginning to feel more confident that they would. They'd survived maybe the most challenging test they would ever face in their lives, by supporting one another. They had fought an entire landscape intent on killing them. They had made friends and learned so much about themselves and about each other. And finally, after so much struggle, after facing down every obstacle in their path, they were on their way.

Below them, the biomes became smaller and smaller, till the entire valley was just a speck. And then that speck was devoured by a continent, and then that continent found its place on that sublime sphere, that tiny blue dot, suspended in the cosmos.

Javi gasped as he looked down on his planet. "Look at how beautiful it is."

As hard as it had all been, he was so grateful to be here in this moment, with his friends. He knew he would never pass this way again.

They had survived it all, and now they were free.

Feather chirped away, and Molly turned to look at them. "She wants to know . . ." Molly took a deep breath. "She needs to know . . . where to? Where would you like to go?"

27

Molly

Home!" Javi said. "That's where she can take us. Home."

"Home . . ." Molly repeated. But she'd hummed the word so Feather could understand.

Even as she said it, it didn't sound right to Molly anymore. She looked down at the color of her skin, the green hue that had overtaken her. She couldn't quite express it to the others, because she knew they wouldn't feel the same way, but she was sad to see the valley collapse. It had tried to kill her friends. It had tried to kill *her*. And yet, somehow, it had begun to feel like home.

She understood the place, in her bones. Just as she'd begun to understand Feather's strange alien tongue. She could communicate with Feather and felt a kinship with her. She even felt at home in this ship that was taking them back to what was *supposed to be* home.

Except Molly knew that it never would be again.

She looked around the ship, at the faces of her friends. They were joyous, relieved, ecstatic to be returning. She didn't want to do anything to take away from that.

But inside, she was conflicted. How could she return back to her old life when she wasn't really human anymore? She had become someone else. And the funny thing was, she *wanted* to embrace her new identity, to dive headlong into it. But how? She wasn't even sure what it might require of her.

Of course she wanted to see her mother, who was wrecked by her father's death. How would her mom grapple with yet another loss? Of course she wanted her feet back on the land that she'd arrived from. But she also understood that she didn't fully belong there anymore, and she didn't know what that meant.

But the others had to return. They had all been through too much.

"Home," Feather repeated in a string of chirps. "And where is that?"

"Take us back to New York," Molly sang to her, until she had to pronounce the city in English. "We flew here from . . ." She grunted in frustration. "New York. America. JFK International Airport." Then, again in birdsong, "That's where we left from, but . . ." She hesitated, turning to the others. "We can't just land at the airport."

"Why not?" Kimberly asked.

"When was the last time you saw a glass flying saucer

arriving at JFK? It's a national security threat. We can't just take an alien spacecraft and land it on the tarmac."

Molly considered how it would all play out. No matter where they landed—in Central Park, on the East River, at Newark Airport, at Citi Field—there would be commotion. An absurd, possibly dangerous, scene would play out for everyone involved. But she wanted to make sure her friends made it home safely.

"I don't think it's a good idea to land at JFK," Javi agreed. "A lot of people in America already think I'm a different kind of alien because of the color of my skin."

"Javi has a point," Anna said. "I'm not sure that the authorities or leadership of our country would make the right decisions to keep us safe."

"We have to accept that no matter where we land, we may not be received well," Molly said to the others. "We might be vilified. We'll *definitely* be interrogated, and I—" Her voice faltered for a moment.

She knew what would be coming for her. In her state, she had to accept the possibility that it might be worse than interrogations. The government would want to run tests on her. She would never be safe.

And it wouldn't end with tests. Even if they somehow decided, definitively, that Molly wasn't a danger to national security, she would still be too different by far. Considering how many people suffered in her own country for being different—for their religious beliefs, or the color of their skin, for being immigrants, for their gender, for loving who they loved—how could they possibly accept her, given the circumstances? A green girl who could speak in birdsong. She wasn't American anymore. She wasn't even Earthly.

"There's one place where we could land that might buy us a little bit of time," Molly said. "No matter where we go, it'll be a madhouse, and we need to be prepared for that. But there's a place in New York where we could land safely and get all of you off this craft."

"All of *us*?" Kimberly asked. "What do you mean, all of us? What about you?"

Molly looked at the faces of her friends before her, landing finally on Javi. Her sweet, loyal, brilliant Javi, who of course had figured it out already. Unlike the others, Javi watched her not with dawning dread, but something closer to resignation.

He knew what she'd been trying to tell him. She didn't need to articulate it.

"After all this, we lose you, too," Javi said softly.

"Don't think of it that way," Molly said to him, to all of them. "It may not be forever. It's just . . . for now. You all saw what happened when Cal and I left the rift. I can't survive here anymore."

Anna grimaced. "If you don't get off this ship with us, where will you even go?"

"With Feather," Molly grated. "Wherever she came from." Molly felt the tears prickling her eyes. Again, her friends were facing yet another loss. As was Molly. By staying on the ship with Feather, she was losing her friends, her family, the place she'd always called home.

And yet it had to be done. Molly wondered if perhaps she had always thought of loss all wrong. Maybe she needed to see it as an offering. She had offered her human self to the rift and become something wondrous. Now she was offering up her old life, in exchange for a new one. One in which she would continue to grow, and thrive, and learn all kinds of new things that she couldn't have learned in her old body, in her old life.

And maybe if she was able to do that, to make this transition gracefully—even if it required some sadness and tears—she might still be able to return one day, when her old world was more ready for her. And when she could survive her old world.

When she turned to face Feather, she knew that her new friend understood everything. Feather had seen her green skin, and the tears in her eyes, and she seemed to know that Molly was ready for the next chapter of her life.

She sang the words to Feather. "One stop," she communicated. Then, in English: "The lawns of the UN, where my friends will be safe."

Feather chirped back at her. "Yes."

"And then—" Molly felt a knot in her throat as she sang. "And then we go home. To your old home. And to my new one. For now."

Feather chirped a lovely birdsong that was only for Molly. She didn't translate the words for the others. "We will welcome you," Feather told her. "Don't worry. We will always keep you safe."

Molly turned to her friends. "Tell my mother that I'm sorry. That I love her. That I miss her. But also that I'm safe. That I'm happy." And she knew when she said the words, they were true.

Anna

Slowly, and then faster and faster, they descended toward Earth, breaking through the atmosphere and the blackness of that endless sky. Then Anna could see it: North America, with its mountains and rivers, its sparkling cities filled with light. There was the East Coast, their home, and then, even closer now, they could see their city. New York City.

The spacecraft dove through a cloud layer before it hovered over the East River. From this height, Anna spotted the High Line, cutting a straight path on the western edge of the city, and there were the Empire State Building and the Flatiron Building, which looked like a tall slice of pie. There was Broadway, cars and buses that zipped across the city like miniature toys. The spaceship turned and crossed westward.

They flew over Central Park, the Guggenheim, the Met. *Home*, Anna kept thinking. Just the word in her mind made her so happy. She hadn't been sure she would ever see it again.

As the ship flew, it cast a shadow over the city. Anna could see people gaping, cars and buses skidding to sudden stops. Small figures ran through the streets, with looks of awe or horror or utter shock on their faces. Arms were pointed to the sky. And then there was that sound that overtook Manhattan like a long wail: alarms and sirens warning people of danger. Helicopters flooded the sky. Finally, Anna could see it approaching: the stately UN Headquarters, perched on the edge of the East River.

The helicopters were still speeding behind them. Just down below, as the shadow of their craft appeared on UN Plaza, Anna could already see crowds forming at the street level. People filled the streets, looking up into the sky, their hands shielding them from the light of the sun as they gazed at the mystery descending from the heavens: a thing they had never seen before.

"How long have we been gone?" Anna asked Molly, who turned to Feather and sang the question.

Feather chirped back and Molly translated. "A month. We've been gone a whole month."

"Feels like a *lot* longer." Javi shook his head in disbelief.

"Not for us," Kimberly said, her eyes wide with anxiety.

"We've been gone almost seventy years. This city . . . I barely recognize it."

Anna and the others hushed into silence.

The ship touched down onto the UN lawn, the glass exterior pressing against thick green grass. Anna and the others were out of their seats in moments, rushing through the ship, their feet echoing through the corridors.

The outer doors had already been opened. In what seemed like no time, Anna found herself standing with her feet on the ground itself, on the Earth again. She scanned the faces of the crowds before them. In their shocked expressions, Anna saw herself reflected back. She could only guess at what they looked like; probably like kids who had just survived hell. All of them except Molly.

Molly.

Anna turned slowly, glancing to the door behind her. Molly stood inside the ship. She smiled, tears in her eyes. Anna grinned back, a heat piercing her own eyes.

Then the doors slid shut. Just as fast as the ship had landed, it was gone again, replaced by the blinding blue and red lights of police cars. Their sirens filled Anna's ears like birdsong—a loud, manic welcome of their city, their home.

They made it. They had returned.

All except Molly.

Yoshi

The next moments were utter confusion. Yoshi didn't know what to say or how to say it. Throngs of people surrounded them: police officers, security guards, even the tourists who had been wandering the lawns of the UN. All of them chattering and looking at him in awe.

It took Yoshi a moment to realize that he was holding something in his hand, an object he didn't even realize had been placed there. But somehow it had, by Feather or the ship, or something else entirely.

"It's a katana," he muttered, holding the blade up to the light. "Except . . . it's different than my old one."

Javi squinted at it. "It looks like it's been 3-D printed, but I don't recognize the material," he said. "Wow, man, that is so cool!"

"It's extremely light," Yoshi said, swiftly cutting the

instrument through the air. The katana Yoshi had lost had been priceless, an heirloom, but perhaps returning with an alien-crafted sword would help soften the blow. It was a blade of two worlds, not unlike him.

Off to Yoshi's side, Akiko squealed. When he turned to look, Yoshi saw the girl was down on her knees. She was . . . *petting* something. A tiny Colossus stood in the grass, not much bigger than a pet pug. Beside her sister, Kira laughed in joy, shaking her head.

Akiko picked up her flute and began to play, and the Colossus responded immediately, spinning in a circle around her. Then she played a trill and the robot turned in a somersault.

"I got something, too," Anna said. She was looking down at a glass tablet in her hand. "It's a . . . I think it's a xenobiology of Feather's planet. It's got images of all these plants and animals. This is amazing . . ."

Javi was next. He was holding a box in his hands, looking down at it with a grin across his face. "It's some kind of a fix-it kit. With alien technology. Oh, man, I am going to have *fun* with this."

In the end, they'd all received something. Hank was given a music box, the tune of which was gentle and sweet. Kira got a set of drawing pigments that changed color with the light. Stu and Drew had some kind of two-way communicators, Dana a container of soothing ointment, and Pammy a clear shield made of superlight glass.

Kimberly's gift was the most mysterious: a strange ring like the antigravity devices that had littered the rift, but with no runes or settings. It took them days to realize that speaking into the ring caused it to erupt in birdsong—in Feather's language. Somehow, she'd given them a translator.

But they didn't have time to explore their gifts just then, standing on the lawn. The crowd had closed in around them, and a series of police officers broke through.

"Uh-oh," Yoshi said. "I guess we have a lot of explaining to do."

30

Anna

How she wanted to be *done* with all this already! How her stomach churned. Anna had been sitting in the interrogation room for hours now, in front of two officials—the secretary of Homeland Security and the commissioner of the NYPD. She was the last one to have to undergo today's interrogation, but they had all been subjected to this sad gray cell. Over the last few weeks, each of them had fielded a slew of questions about where they'd been and what they'd seen. They were being treated like criminals by their own government.

"I'm telling you," Anna explained patiently. "Molly's taken off. She's visiting Feather's planet."

"And can you describe this . . . Feather person to us again?" the commissioner asked, cocking her head to one side.

Anna sighed at the woman sitting across from her. Her

name was Patricia Widen, and in the last few weeks Anna had become more familiar with her face than she was with her own.

Typically, Commissioner Widen played the role of good cop, whereas the secretary of Homeland Security, a man named Brett Kurten with a meaty, pasty face, simply barked things at her.

Anna fidgeted in her seat. "Feather is . . . an avian creature. Or something near enough to it. I'm not sure how you'd taxonomize a convergent evolution from another planet. Her world . . . well, she called it 'nest.' That's where Molly went. To the nest. After she brought us here. On that flying saucer you saw?"

"And you really expect us to believe that?" Kurten raised his voice.

"You *saw* the spacecraft." Anna shook her head and laughed. "If not in person, then definitely on TV. You know about the plane crash. What exactly do you think I'm hiding?"

"I can think of plenty," he ground out. Anna waited for him to elaborate, but of course he didn't. She was tired of the grown-ups who acted this way. As though they knew she was keeping some dark secret from them—had already figured it out, in fact, and all they needed was for her to confess. Really they were just overgrown children.

Kurten was playing detective. Anna didn't always express herself in the ways that she wished, but she was more of an adult than *him*.

"My guess is you've gotten the same story from all my friends," she said. "What reason would we have to lie to you?" She actually rolled her eyes at him. Before everything she'd been through with the others, a man like this—an entitled, know-it-all, aggressive jerk—might have frightened her. Now very little truly scared Anna. She'd faced so many of her fears in the rift.

"What reason? What *reason*?" He emphasized the last word, saying it slowly. Even though Anna wasn't always good at picking up social cues, she had the impression he was stalling.

"Yeah," she said flatly. "What reason?" She shrugged.

"You could be a domestic terrorist. Maybe you blew up that plane."

Anna laughed aloud. "I'm a high school student. And I'd like to return to being one. Are you sure you're the secretary of Homeland Security? What did you do before this?" She scrunched up her face. "Were you the president's party planner? Or maybe a concierge at one of his hotels? Are you . . . actually qualified to do this job?"

Commissioner Widen cleared her throat. "Anna, we're not trying to scare you. We just want to collect as much information as we possibly can. Did this Feather tell you anything about her planet?"

Anna shook her head, thinking sadly of Molly. "Only that it's far away. And that it's very technologically advanced. When her ship crashed in the Arctic, it created a number of biomes reminiscent of her world. But they were all swallowed when the rift collapsed. And by now, you've interrogated all of us, so you should have all this information already." Anna looked at the door before her. "Can I go home now?"

Anna wanted her family. And she was looking forward to talking to Yoshi again. His parents had been relieved to find him alive, just as her own parents had doubled over in joy, tears flowing from their eyes when they first came to collect her from the UN. Yoshi's parents had told him he could stay wherever he wanted: in New York with his mother or in Tokyo with his father. He'd decided to stay in New York. Anna suspected she had something to do with his decision, and she was relieved. Having Yoshi in her life made her happy.

The others had been reunited with their parents as well: Javi's entire family had come to collect him the day they landed on the UN lawn, his mom and dad, his brothers and sisters. They brought food and blankets for all the kids, wrapping them up and wiping away tears.

Javi's mother had turned to Anna's mom. "We're all family now. After everything we've been through, everything *they've* been through together." And she was right. They had their own tribe now, their own little village. They had experienced something extraordinary together, and no amount of bullying questioning was going to change that.

Molly's mom had been hit the hardest. She hadn't even been able to see Molly before she took off, though Anna had relayed Molly's message to her. Tears had sprung from her eyes when Anna spoke the words. It was so unfair, all the losses she had suffered. And yet, Anna hoped she felt some solace in knowing that Molly was seeing something no living creature from Earth ever had.

Anna wondered if she would ever see her friend again. She missed Molly. Hopefully one day, she would return.

Perhaps Anna would be old by then, and it would be somewhat like the Cub-Tones reuniting with their friends. Anna had helped Kimberly, Hank, and the others reconnect with a handful of people from their old lives in Bear Claw, Oregon. Some lived in nursing homes now, and if all went well, the Cub-Tones would be flying there in the next few months to visit.

Kimberly, especially, had been flabbergasted by the internet. A way to communicate instantly with people so far away! She'd wiped her eyes when they closed the video chat window. "We missed an entire lifetime here on Earth," she mused, shock in her voice.

"But we have an entirely new lifetime to live," Hank said. He had been more optimistic since their return, riding the excitement of everything's *newness*. The entire world had changed in their absence. People had iPhones now, and cable TV, and Instagram, and hybrid vehicles.

Javi's parents had made the decision to foster the Cub-Tones, and they took in Molly's mom as well, in her grief. They were all staying in New York, which was good because Anna and Yoshi and the others would see them on a regular basis. Even Akiko and Kira's parents had eventually relented, agreeing to let the twins return to the city twice a year to visit. They all needed each other.

Anna had learned what was important during her time in the rift. The Earth was important. Her life was important. Her friends were important. Her family was important.

The man sitting before her, bullying her into giving the answers he wanted to hear, wasn't important.

"Listen," she said to him now. "Whatever it is you're looking for, I don't think you're going to find it here in some sham of an interview. I'm also guessing my friends have all told you the same thing. So you might as well let me go."

"Excuse me?" Kurten asked her, his face turning crimson. "Who do you think you are?"

She threw her shoulders back. "I'm Anna. I spent a month in an alien rift in the Arctic. I survived because of the brilliance of my friends. And my own brilliance."

"Oh!" He laughed in her face. "So now you think you're brilliant?"

"I think I'm brilliant and enterprising and kind and open and good. I also think I'm a media darling right now. Not only are we the survivors of Aero Horizon Flight 16, we have publicly proven the existence of extraterrestrial life. So unless you and the president want the entire country—the entire world—turning against you, what you're going to do right now is let me walk out that door."

Kurten leaned back in his chair. "Is that what you think?"

"It's what I know."

"Then *I* think we're done here." Commissioner Widen actually winked at her!

Kurten's neck snapped around so quickly, Anna half worried he'd injure himself. "You're ready to just let her *go*?"

Patricia Widen smiled at Anna and nodded. That was all the signal Anna needed. She got up and walked to the door, pushed it open, and exited into the maze of halls. Minutes later, she was outside the building and into the streets of New York, where Yoshi was waiting for her. They were meeting at a corner diner for sundaes with Kimberly and Hank and the others.

The Cub-Tones loved diners. They reminded them of another time, a time that no longer existed.

But that was the thing about life in general. You were in a moment and then, all of a sudden, the moment was gone. Anna wanted to make the most of the moments she had left. She wanted to make the most of her life. She wanted to love her friends and her family. She wanted to be a scientist. She wanted to make this planet better. She wanted to leave something—an idea, a discovery—behind.

And she would do it. They all would. They were so very different from the people who'd first entered the rift. They were becoming the people they were meant to be.

And that was the best that anyone could ask for.